DORSEY KELLEY

Montana Heat

Published by Silhouette Books New York

America's Publisher of Contemporary Romance

To Bob,
my romantic inspiration.

And to Stacey, Kel and Sony—
for just everything.

SILHOUETTE BOOKS
300 E. 42nd St., New York, N.Y. 10017

Copyright © 1990 by Dorsey Adams

All rights reserved. Except for use in any review, the reproduction or utilization of this work in whole or in part in any form by any electronic, mechanical or other means, now known or hereafter invented, including xerography, photocopying and recording, or in any information storage or retrieval system, is forbidden without the permission of Silhouette Books, 300 E. 42nd St., New York, N.Y. 10017

ISBN: 0-373-08714-4

First Silhouette Books printing April 1990

All the characters in this book are fictitious. Any resemblance to actual persons, living or dead, is purely coincidental.

®: Trademark used under license and registered in the United States Patent and Trademark Office and in other countries.

Printed in the U.S.A.

"You're a maverick, aren't you, Nick?"

Tracy paused in the doorway. "You don't bother with such silly conventions as attempting to be *nice* or *accommodating* or even *courteous*. Oh, no. Not you."

"I'll tell you one thing, Miss California," Nick said softly. "I am different from other men in one way. I'm sure as hell not getting suckered into believing myths about women."

"What myths?"

With a savage twist he ground out the butt of his cigarette in an ashtray. "That some of you are special. Which damn well isn't so. You're all alike—you women. You all run off when things get sticky. Like now. Trouble is, you aren't *man* enough to stand here and talk this out."

She glared at him. "I'm not running off."

Dear Reader,

Happy Spring! April 1990 is in full bloom—the crocuses are bursting forth, the trees are beginning to bud and though we have an occasional inclement wind, as Shelley wrote in *Ode to the West Wind*, "O Wind, If Winter comes, can Spring be far behind?"

And in this special month of nature's rebirth, we have some wonderful treats in store for you. Silhouette Romance's DIAMOND JUBILEE is in full swing, and this month discover *Harvey's Missing* by Peggy Webb, a delightful romp about a man, a woman and a lovable dog named Harvey (aka George). Then, in May, love is in the air for heroine Lara MacEuan and her handsome, enigmatic hero, Miles Crane, in *Second Time Lucky* by Victoria Glenn.

The DIAMOND JUBILEE—Silhouette Romance's tenth anniversary celebration—is our way of saying thanks to you, our readers. To symbolize the timelessness of love, as well as the modern gift of the tenth anniversary, we're presenting readers with a DIAMOND JUBILEE Silhouette Romance title each month, penned by one of your favorite Silhouette Romance authors. In the coming months, writers such as Marie Ferrarella, Lucy Gordon, Dixie Browning, Phyllis Halldorson—to name just a few—are writing DIAMOND JUBILEE titles especially for you.

And that's not all! Pepper Adams has written a wonderful trilogy—*Cimarron Stories*—set on the plains of Oklahoma. And Laurie Paige has a heartwarming duo coming up—*Homeward Bound*. Be sure to look for them in late spring/early summer. Much-loved Diana Palmer also has some special treats in store during the months ahead....

I hope you'll enjoy this book and all of the stories to come. Come home to romance—Silhouette Romance—for always!

Sincerely,

Tara Hughes Gavin
Senior Editor

DORSEY KELLEY

claims she has loved and read romance novels forever and can't bear to throw one away. Hence, she has books stuck into every cranny of her house. Her interests include romping with her three small daughters, tennis and a good bottle of champagne shared with her husband. She lives near the coast in Southern California.

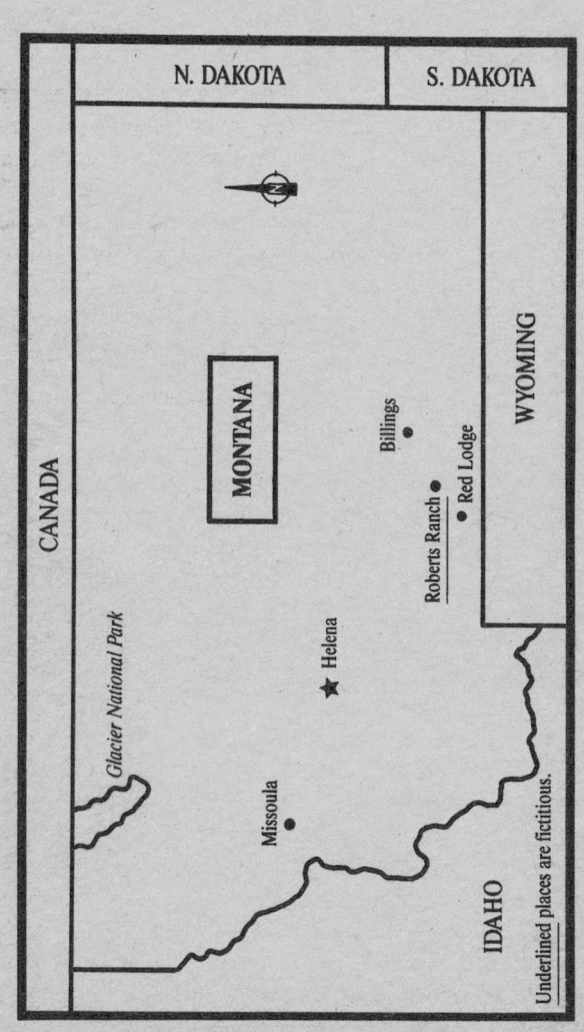

Chapter One

Nick Roberts waited his turn, one scuffed and booted heel resting on the bottom rail of the rodeo arena as he watched Billy Roy Jenkins get peeled from the saddle of the meanest bronc this side of the Pecos. Nick grinned broadly. His turn would be up soon and then he'd show them. Show 'em all—eager crowds and fellow buckaroos alike—that Nick Roberts was tough as mesquite and ornery as any bronc in Montana.

From the top of his Stetson-clad head to the dusty Western shirt that molded his shoulders, from corded arms to hip-snug jeans, Nick spelled cowboy. And if anyone cared to take a second look, they would see the deep crescent-shaped scar twisting across his right forearm and the slightly bow-legged stance that had become an integral part of him.

Nick ground out a half-smoked cigarette beneath his heel then draped his arms over the rail. Four more riders to go and he would be up. With tense fingers he yanked another cigarette from his breast pocket and cupped his hands around a match. Inhaling once, he squinted through the smoke, then ground out that cigarette, too. Nick wondered at his tension. Maybe he was getting too old for this sort of thing—certainly most of the other saddle-bronc riders were in their teens and early twenties. With a muffled oath he swore under his breath. Hell, twenty-eight was still young. If he was any judge, he had several good years left on the circuit.

Cowboy was what he was, and rodeoing was what he lived for. Neither man nor beast nor woman had ever come between them, by damn. Cynically, he took in an eyeful of the prancing buckle bunnies who waited by the small outer gate for the rodeo stars. More than a few returned his interested glance. They were a fine-looking lot, too, he decided, noting the purple-fringed suede skirt and matching boots outfitting one striking redhead. All the girls were gaudily dressed, each nurturing the hope of outshining the others with her showy outfit. All but one.

A small blonde, she rested her arms on the arena rail much as he did, but her slight stature enabled her to reach only the second rung. Instead of giggling and trying to catch his eye, she ignored him, watching the proceedings inside the ring with avid interest.

Her clothing was much too plain, Nick thought, somehow impatient with her for the oversight. Instead of that generic brand of jeans, she ought to have one of those designer numbers that cupped a woman's hips and thighs so a man could see what he was getting. She certainly had the figure for it. Her muted-plaid blouse, though it couldn't hide the generous swell of her bosom, ought to be unbuttoned at least two more down—the way a man liked. Her hair wasn't quite right, either. Pretty, shining shade of palomino though it was, it ought not be pulled back in that fancy braid, but allowed to spill free about her shoulders.

Nick shook his head. She'd learn. When the buckaroos passed her by in favor of ones dressed like the redhead in purple, she would figure it out soon enough. He shook his head again, but then caught his breath in surprise.

Drawn perhaps by his scrutiny, she turned and looked directly at him. Wide and questioning, her dark-fringed hazel eyes studied him. Without any obvious intent to flirt, her curious gaze flicked over him, pausing a brief moment on the scar on his arm. But her gaze was impersonal, as if she were inspecting one of the horses.

Nick's amusement and discomfort growing in equal amounts, he was about to grin back when she turned again toward the ring, her chin tilted and her little nose pointed in the air. Clearly she was far more interested in the rodeo than him.

Strangely, he felt bereft...and annoyed. He didn't know how or why, but the feeling that he'd failed some test angered him. He wasn't at the very top of his profession—not anymore—but he'd ridden respectably for a good ten years. He'd even won the National Finals Rodeo at Oklahoma City once and had the belt buckle to prove it. Dammit, he was good, with nothing to be ashamed of, and it rankled him more than he cared to admit that some bit of fluff like her was looking down her nose at him.

It wasn't until she turned to frown at him that he heard his name called for the second time. In ill humor he stomped over to the chute, climbed up and lowered himself onto the back of the piebald gelding. Eager to prove himself more than ever, Nick gripped the rope rein in his left hand and nodded for the attendant to open the chute.

* * *

Tracy Wilborough watched the cowboy wrap his long legs around the piebald with a kind of fascinated horror. What could the man be thinking of, to climb onto the back of a half-crazed animal whose only purpose in life was to rid itself of the unwelcome burden? What kind of man did it take to risk life and limb day in and out—and for what? Mere money and applause and more scars to match the one he already had?

The other cowboys waiting their turns or nursing bruises from their own rides sang out good-natured catcalls as the rider raked his spurs over the gelding from shoulder to rump. And the brightly clad cluster of women stopped prancing for a moment to watch.

Shooting high in the air and then twisting down, the piebald fought the man with fierce intent. Billowing dust thrown up by furious hooves choked Tracy and burned her eyes. The gelding bellowed and grunted, outraged. Tracy wanted to call her three boys who were somewhere close by to watch the fascinating battle. But she knew the ride would last only eight seconds and she was powerless to drag her eyes away.

The horse ducked his head between his forelegs and let loose with a series of bone-jarring leaps that tossed the man about, making him look more like a ragdoll than a man. Yet still the cowboy hung on.

These men, Tracy concluded, were decidedly mad.

The judges' bell sounded and the pickup riders moved in to release the bucking strap and yank the cowboy off. Once on the ground, he threw a cocky salute to the cheering crowd, and Tracy caught her breath as the piebald's still-flying hooves barely missed his head. He was either too arrogant to take notice or too foolish to steer clear. Either way, Tracy felt her irritation rise.

Life, she'd learned over the past eighteen months, was much too precious to gamble. Since Craig's death she'd had a lot of time to reflect on it. Craig had loved fast cars. He'd been an adequate husband and a fair daddy to their three, but his love for cars had cost him his life in the end. Now, studying the rough cowboy as he bowed to the audience, Tracy realized her anger with Craig for getting himself killed in that accident had yet to dissipate. He'd left her a widow, darn it, a widow and a single parent to boot. Now everything they'd done together she had to do alone, take out the trash alone, make all the decisions alone, go to bed...alone.

Sighing, Tracy let her gaze fall on her youngest, two-and-a-half-year-old Toby. Her game little towhead was doing his best to keep up with Brady and Dan, eight and seven, as they ran toward her.

"Mom!" Brad yelled, excitement raising the pitch of his voice. "Did you see 'em? Did you? Mom, those guys can really ride."

"Really ride!" Dan echoed from behind.

Brady grabbed her arm. "Is that how it was when you were growing up, Mom? Did you get to go to a lot of rodeos?"

Hating to disappoint them, Tracy said gently, "Some. But that was a long time ago. And Grandma and Grandpa's spread was more like a farm than the ranch we'll be living on now." She tousled their heads, noting idly that the pickup men were having trouble corraling the still-bucking piebald. From the corner of her eye she caught sight of an approaching man.

Tall and slim, David Roberts smiled at Tracy. A small blond girl holding a dripping snow cone perched on his right hip and a boy of about nine trailed behind him.

Tracy gave a rueful shake of her head. All these kids. Five children! How was she to manage? David had seemed impressed with her meager credentials—she'd once worked as a teacher at a preschool. Ever since she'd answered his ad for a nanny, he'd acted delighted that she was a mother herself. A perfect nanny, he wrote. Somehow he'd viewed her motherhood as another credential instead of a liability, as she'd discovered most employers were wont to do. Apparently, he hoped his children and hers would be friends since his ranch was somewhat remote from others. Tracy hoped they would, too.

She chuckled to herself. She hoped she'd be able to pull this job off. If she was lucky, David would think she knew all the answers and maybe never discover she was muddling through just like every other parent.

Now, looking at the little girl's sticky smile behind the snow cone, Tracy felt her customary confidence return. She *would* succeed at this job. She loved children—she loved teaching them, playing with them, caring for them. She also needed the work; Craig's modest financial legacy had almost run out.

"Did you see them?" David shifted the girl to his other hip, unknowingly repeating her son's question and eager tone. But then he surprised Tracy by asking, "Did you see my brother?"

"Brother? I didn't know you had one." Confused, Tracy glanced around at the milling crowds.

"Of course! He's why we're here today."

"He is?"

David smiled. "I'm sorry. I guess I forgot to mention it this morning. When you arrived and we were leaving for the rodeo, well, we hadn't expected you till tomorrow and everything was so hectic—"

"You shouldn't have felt as though you had to invite us," Tracy put in quickly. She still felt awkward about arriving a day early and surprising David and his family. Somehow she'd gotten the dates confused, and she *had* been so anxious to get to Montana....

"Nonsense. Glad you're here. Anyway, I can introduce you to Nick now, since he's coming this way."

Tracy swung around toward the arena. The piebald was still giving the now irritated pickup men the slip. But the only man bearing down on them seemed to be the reckless cowboy, coming across the arena after retrieving his fallen hat and dusting it off on his thigh. Tracy watched, a sinking premonition insisting that this arrogant cowboy was David's brother.

As the man closed the gap, Tracy saw he was almost swaggering. Jamming the Stetson far back on his head, the cowboy's wide grin revealed a slash of white on the tanned, weathered canvas of his face. His jeans, soft and faded, clung to his slightly bowed legs and fit snugly around hips banded by a leather belt decorated with a flashy silver buckle. Across his right forearm the deep scar she'd noticed earlier snaked from elbow almost to wrist, disfiguring the smooth muscled contour.

His face held little of David's handsomeness. With features too roughly hewn and cockily arrogant for her taste, he didn't appeal to her on any level except one of irritation. Sourly, Tracy thought it was too bad he was David's brother; with his recklessness he wouldn't be a good role model for the children.

He reached for the gate latch in front of them. But over his shoulder, Tracy had the brief impression of the excited horse—nostrils flared with snorted breaths—headed straight across the arena. A thousand-plus pounds of wild-eyed horseflesh thundered toward them and Tracy was standing in the open gate. Then, before she could react to the danger bearing down on her, the man exploded into violent action. With a muffled shout, he leaped through the opening.

He slammed the gate shut behind himself and crashed into her, knocking the air from her lungs. She sprawled in the dirt, the man solidly atop her. Out of breath, Tracy knew only shock and the pain of his weight crushing her into the hard earth. His big belt buckle ground into her hip.

Rougher than seemed necessary, the man eased his bulk off Tracy and with a calloused hand thrust her head between her legs, holding it there until at last blessed air was returned to her in a gulping rush. Frightened and enraged, she gasped, glaring at him from the inelegant position. The smell of saddle leather and sweat assailed her nostrils. He sat beside her, his long legs bent at the knees, booted feet on the ground, giving her a rueful grin.

"Well, now, I'm real sorry 'bout this, ma'am. Guess I was in a hurry to get out the gate and sorta plowed over you." His lazy, low-timbered drawl floated over Tracy in unconcerned tones, erasing nost of her fear but leaving the fury.

"Here, let me help you up." He hauled her to a shaky standing position and began dusting her off, beginning with her back and ending, shockingly, by patting the dust from her derriere. "It looked like it was either me or that bronc in there, and any way you look at it, I'm lighter. You ought not hang around these gates, you know."

"Oh!" Tracy pushed his hands away in annoyance. "Why didn't you avoid me, leaping out of the gate like that? Why didn't you—"

"Mom! Are you all right?" Brady said anxiously as he rushed up with the others. "That cowboy saved you!"

"You all right?" seconded Dan.

"Mawww," wailed Toby, beginning to cry.

"I'm fine, boys. I just had the air knocked out of me. I'll be okay." She lifted Toby, cuddling him reassuringly. Over the boy's head she sent the cowboy an accusing glare.

"I see you've met already." David chuckled after assuring himself Tracy was unhurt. "However, let me make it formal. Tracy Wilborough, meet the best saddle-bronc rider in these parts, sometime rancher and my brother, Nicholas Roberts. Nick, the woman you just barreled into is the new nanny—come all the way from California to care for the kids."

If he expects me to shake his hand he's in for a big surprise, Tracy thought to herself. But Nick robbed her of the pleasure of ignoring his outstretched hand when he merely tipped his hat.

His easy grin vanished. "I hope she's more careful of the kids' safety than she is of her own," he growled. Disapproval and some measure of hostility came into his tobacco-brown eyes, the corners of which crinkled in a scowl. He stood there, legs spread wide, one hand negligently resting on a lean hip—inspecting her. "And in the future, stay clear of me when I'm riding—I don't have time for rescuing women."

Tracy drew in a quick, surprised breath. The insulting words and his aggressive expression took her off guard. What in God's name had *she* done? He'd been the one acting like a brute when a simple "get out of way" would have sufficed.

Nick studied Tracy Wilborough without blinking. So, she wasn't one of the buckle bunnies, but a . . . a *nanny* who would live in his house for God's sake. Damn! That's all the family needed now—some cute little cookie to complicate all their lives. A divorcée, he guessed, and not more than twenty-eight or nine, with three kids of her own to further clutter his life if the young pups crowding around were hers. Well, hell, she'd probably jumped at answering David's ad. What woman alone in her position wouldn't want to live on a prestigious Montana cattle ranch—rent free—and maybe hook the wealthy rancher in the process?

Nick swore under his breath, noting the bewildered look that came to her face at his crack about the kids' safety. A good actress, too. He controlled the urge to shake her, tell her to get her tail back to California before she caused them any trouble. Too bad he hadn't knocked some sense into her when he'd mowed her down. David, in the grip of vulnerable emotions, would most likely fall for Tracy like a ton of bricks. Nick swept his gaze over her trim thighs and hips, past her rounded breasts to linger on her wide, hazel eyes and full, sensuous lips. Her honey-gold hair glistened in the sunlight. Yep, like a ton of bricks.

Gathering herself, Tracy knew only a strong desire to put one Nicholas Roberts in his place. "I certainly don't want to be anywhere *near* you when you're riding," Tracy told him belatedly. "A woman is in serious danger when you're in the ring." She had the satisfaction of seeing an angry flush stain his tanned cheeks. Before he could speak, she turned to David, who grinned broadly at her words.

"I'll take Kitty now," she said stiffly, holding out her arms for the sticky little girl. "Let's go to the ladies' room and get cleaned up, okay?" Without a backward glance at either man, she led Kitty and Toby off.

As the day wore on the foreboding Tracy experienced since being introduced to Nick Roberts grew. With some shock she learned David's ranch, where she and the boys would be living, along with an Aunt Millie, belonged to Nick as well. Since fall roundup on the cattle ranch would begin in a matter of weeks, Nick would leave the rodeo circuit and live at home to help. And the rodeo today in Red Lodge was almost his last of the year.

Tracy watched him swing his niece into his arms so she could see the roping contest inside the ring. He smiled as Kitty squealed in delight, and then discussed the merits of different roping techniques with his nephew. Apparently his remoteness was reserved only for her.

By the end of the day Tracy had decided polite indifference would be the best tack. But as she discovered on the way home, being sandwiched between the door and Nick in David's double-cabbed truck, polite indifference was difficult to maintain.

"Comfortable?" Nick asked, letting his gaze roam over her thighs, which were obviously wedged quite uncomfortably against him and the door handle.

"Perfectly," she replied, managing a brilliant smile. Nick's large frame pressed along the length of her left side, and attempts to draw away were futile. Scents of sweat and smoke and saddle leather clung to Nick, and Tracy knew these particular smells would cling to her now, too.

David put the truck into gear and bumped over the fairground's dirt road leading to the highway. Because Nick's wide shoulders overlapped hers, his elbow poked accidentally into her breast. Face burning, Tracy caught Nick's lazy grin slanting down at her.

She crossed her arms, wondering if he'd ever heard of personal space and if he knew he was invading hers.

She didn't know why he didn't appear to like her. They hardly knew each other. But his reasons were fast becoming unimportant because she was learning to dislike him, as well.

He'd been rough, rude and cynically mocking in the short time since she'd met him. What she needed now was a barrier—something to distance her from his lanky frame that was too close, too big and too disturbing. Toby, making a nuisance of himself in the front seat beside Kyle, provided a welcome diversion.

"Come sit on Mommy's lap, sweetie." She held out her arms to the boy, but to her chagrin, Nick hauled Toby onto his own lap. Instead of shying away from intimate contact with a stranger, as Toby *always* did, he sat quietly, awestruck, across the cowboy's knees.

"Big hat," Toby said, pointing a chubby finger at the rawhide-colored Stetson that sat far back on Nick's head.

"You like that, don't you, partner?" Nick grinned engagingly and set the hat on Toby's head.

"Darling," Tracy tried, "don't you want to come here, on Mommy's lap?"

Toby shook his head vehemently, happy fingers playing over the brim of the huge Stetson. "Like big hat."

"Can I try it on?" Brady asked from Nick's other side.

"Can I?" Dan echoed.

"Sure, sure. But you're going to live on a ranch now, boys. We'd best get you all hats of your own."

"Really?" Dan said in awe, and Tracy sighed to herself as Nick launched into a tall tale of harsh life on the range, rugged cowboys riding line shacks in winter and eating "grub" under the stars. In short order Tracy's boys were utterly captivated. But she didn't interfere. The kids needed something to keep them occupied on the drive home, although she didn't believe a word of Nick's stories.

His tales grew more unbelievable, the feats of the cowboys more heroic, and in turn, her boys grew increasingly enthralled. In the middle of a particularly unbelievable story, Nick slanted Tracy a wicked grin, as if daring her to challenge him. She met his gaze, lending her chin an impudent tilt.

But something happened. She saw his big rough hand, so gentle with her little boy, saw a bit of good-natured *come-laugh-with-me* humor in his grin, and something exchanged between them in that instant, an affinity that Tracy had never before experienced with another man. Her skin felt hot all over and confusion overwhelmed her.

She dropped her gaze, oddly shy, but then raised it again to meet his. He looked dazed, as if struck by the same lightning bolt of attraction.

With the suddenness of an unexpected chinook descending to melt a midwinter snow, Tracy knew Nick Roberts would most certainly complicate her life.

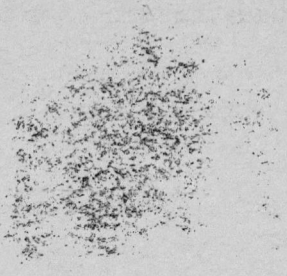

Chapter Two

"I realize *nanny* is an old-fashioned word," David said to Tracy after a delicious dinner served by his elderly Aunt Millie. The children were watching television in the next room while Tracy discussed the terms of her employment with David. His office was large, its book-lined walls and heavy, masculine furniture suiting him. David sat on a soft leather sofa, Tracy on a huge wing chair covered with subtly striped maroon fabric.

He crossed an ankle over his other knee, continuing, "But as I explained in my letter, a nanny is exactly what we need. At nine, Kyle really just needs supervision. He'll have to be driven to school, with your boys, of course, when fall semester begins. Kitty, well, with a two-year-old of your own, you already know what she needs—to be dressed properly, bathed, played with—you know."

"Of course." Tracy smiled, imagining sunny afternoon tea parties, clothing the little girl in frilly dresses, plaiting her golden hair. "I'm looking forward to caring for Kitty especially. She seems so gentle and loving—not at all rough-and-tumble like the boys."

David nodded, his open face showing complete understanding. "Girls are special, that's for sure." He smiled. "We're happy to have you, Tracy. I spend as much time with the kids as I can—but I do have to run the ranch. Since Eliza's been gone, we've needed help." A shadow passed over his face as he mentioned his wife's name. Then he appeared to shake himself. "Aunt Millie does a fine job keeping house, but she's getting on in years, you understand. She doesn't have the energy to chase the kids *and* keep house."

Nodding, Tracy recognized the end of the interview. She rose, saying warmly, "Thank you for hiring me. I grew up on a small ranch in California. Nothing like this—" she gestured with her hands "—but we had a few horses and farm animals. I've always had a yearning to return to my roots, so to speak. I love it here, already."

"That's good."

"If it's all right, I'd like to have a look around the house. It's been decorated beautifully."

David frowned, the shadow appearing again. Faint lines of strain appeared at the edges of his eyes. He had an air, she realized, of deep-rooted unhappiness. "Yes," he said. "Eliza did it. Anyway, feel free. Consider this your home now, too."

Tracy moved away, her heart going with great empathy to the saddened rancher. She knew what it was to lose a spouse. She knew the agony. The engulfing sadness. The despair.

Swallowing, she forced herself to shake off her depressing thoughts. Wasn't that why she'd come to Montana—to escape her smothering, well-meaning friends, the familiar house and furnishings, everything that reminded her of her life with Craig?

Come on, Wilborough, he's been gone eighteen months! she scolded inwardly, striding down the hallway toward the kitchen. It was time to get on with her life. Not to forget Craig, but to forgive him for dying.

Just as she turned to enter the saloon-style swinging doors of Millie's kitchen, Tracy caught sight of herself in a large gilt-edged wall mirror. Her reflection revealed an unfamiliar pallor and an uncharacteristic thinness, showing she hadn't regained the pounds she'd lost after the funeral.

Taking a deep breath, Tracy drew herself up. She was here. It had taken courage to uproot herself and her children from their home in California and travel east to an unknown ranch and uncertain future.

But she'd made it. She'd done the right thing. Her usually robust health needed a good dose of serenity and fresh air. She'd gambled her children's happiness, as well as her own, on the move. It was the right thing to do. Of course it was. The only person who hadn't been all kindness was David's brother, Nick. But Tracy had counted too much on finding peace to let one man's grumpy personality spoil things. She just wished he didn't disturb her so.

In the knotty-pine paneled kitchen, she found Aunt Millie bent over a soapy sinkful of dishes. Tracy greeted her, collected a towel and began drying.

Millie wore her dark hair, liberally streaked with gray, piled into a haphazard topknot. Her bright brown eyes sparkled and her gestures were quick and efficient. On sizing Tracy up at their first meeting, she'd patted the younger woman on the cheek and smiled, saying only, "You'll do."

Tracy was grateful Millie had extended her welcome so easily. She was glad there would be somebody to liven the days, particularly since learning she would share the house with a man like Nick Roberts. At this juncture in her life, she thought ruefully, she needed to be around *someone* with a congenial disposition.

She swiped her damp towel over another plate and began, "Millie—"

"*Aunt* Millie."

Tracy grinned. "Aunt Millie. This house is fabulous. I've always liked the Southern-mansion-style home. When you come up the driveway, those white pillars are impressive. We don't get much of this type of architecture in California."

A dreamy look flitted across Millie's face. "Yes. My brother built it for his bride—David and Nick's mother—some thirty-eight years ago."

"She must have loved it."

Inexplicably, Millie sighed, her mouth puckering at some remembered sorrow. "One would have thought so."

At a loss, Tracy tried, "Well, I'm sure Eliza was happy with it."

After a pause that felt too long and a deepening frown from Millie, the other woman shrugged. "I guess she liked decorating it, anyway."

"Oh." There were undercurrents here that Tracy could only guess at—and a lot she didn't understand. But it wasn't her place to start asking personal questions.

However, she was entitled to some background. "I'm sure Kitty and Kyle miss their mother terribly. When did she pass away?"

"*Pass away!*" Abruptly, Millie straightened, frothy suds dripping from her elbows.

Beginning to wish she'd chosen to talk about the weather, the stock market, anything but the women of the house, Tracy bit her lip. Uncomfortable, she tugged at the collar of her plaid shirt. "Yes, well, hasn't Eliza... I mean, isn't she... um...?"

"Dead?" Millie barked. "Heavens, no! Who on earth told you that?"

"In the ad... that is, David wrote he was a widower looking for a nanny."

Her frown fading, Millie chuckled. She resumed washing dishes with renewed vigor. "That rascal, David. Can't entirely blame him. I guess it wouldn't look too good in the newspaper for him to have written, 'Abandoned husband needs woman to care for kids.'"

Tracy set the last plate in the cupboard and hung the dishtowel on the counter with studied care. "No," she replied numbly, "I guess not."

"Don't worry. David probably figured you might not come if you knew his wife had simply left him. He's got his pride, Tracy. Not in the stubborn, hotheaded way like Nicholas. But quietlike." She touched her breast. "Inside. You don't really mind about Eliza, do you?"

"Of course not," Tracy hastened to assure her. "But—whatever happened?" The words came blurting out, too fast to stop, and Tracy could do nothing to take them back.

But Millie didn't appear offended at the personal question. She snatched up Tracy's damp towel and began wiping the tiled countertop. "Guess it won't hurt for you to know. You'll be living here now, you got a right. See, David married a city girl. Career-woman type." Millie shrugged. "Nothing wrong with that—except somewhere along the line he and Eliza imagined a different path for their marriage. He figured she'd stay at home having babies and keeping his house. She wanted to go on working."

"I guess that made for problems."

"Sure did."

"But why did she wait so long? They must have been married at least ten years."

"Eleven." Millie sighed, leaning an ample hip on the counter. "At first she wanted to quit work. But after Kyle was born she got the urge to go back. Can't say as I blame her. She had a college degree in interior design. A body'd want to get some use out of all that schooling. That's when the arguments started. She and David compromised when they agreed she could renovate this old house."

"She did a terrific job. I love all the hardwood flooring and the way the drapes match the sofas and cushions. She's really talented."

"Yep. But when the house was done, Kitty was born and the arguments started up again. Finally, it got so bad she just left. That was four months ago." She shook her head. "Nick's been the very devil to live with since then."

"Nick? Why would *he* be—of course, he'd be upset for his brother, but . . ."

"Don't listen to me, I'm just an old chatterbox."

"Do you mean—Oh, Millie, you can't be saying Nick and Eliza were—"

"No! Nick would never hurt David that way. And Eliza and David love each other. No question about that. Besides, although Eliza and Nick get along fine, I don't think she's his type. Let's just say that Nick and David's mother was no saint. Then, with Eliza deserting his brother like that—well, Nick takes things hard. That boy's got a good heart, make no mistake. But I guess he figures he's got reason not to trust women."

Tracy thought about that for a moment, then, with the kitchen clean and dishes put away, she found her excuse for quizzing Millie had evaporated. She left, searching out a sleepy Kitty and protesting Toby, and by tactful suggestion and some enticing bribes of going to see the "horsies" tomorrow, got them both to bed.

Upstairs, there was no dearth of bedrooms. David had generously offered a separate room for each boy and for herself, but she found Brady and Dan didn't want to be alone. Staying in the same room probably reinforced a feeling of security in the unfamiliar house, Tracy thought, smiling to herself. Though her boys sometimes fought like two cats with their tails tied together, she knew each held a strong brotherly love in his heart for the other.

Constructed in a lazy L, the home's many bedrooms were all upstairs. Long, wide hallways, brightened by tiny-print wallpaper and an oak chair railing, connected them. Downstairs, the front room, or "parlor" as Millie called it, opened from the huge front double doors. The family room, which housed a wide-screen television and several comfortable sofas and easy chairs, served as a place to relax. The wet bar with gleaming brass sink comprised part of one wall. Hunting scenes and paintings by Charles M. Russell depicting ferocious Indians pursuing shaggy bison decorated the walls. Everything blended together to create a homey, yet well-appointed estate.

Never had Tracy been in such a magnificent house. Nor had she expected to actually *live* in one. As she tucked a finally unprotesting Toby in his new bed and saw her older boys, as well as Kyle and Kitty, safely behind the closed doors of theirs, Tracy took in a deep breath. Tired, she leaned her back against the wall outside Brady and Dan's room and rubbed her forehead. She was lucky to be here.

Her new life was well and truly begun. Now, it was to be seen if she could make a success of it, or if she'd muddle it up as she had her life with Craig. Though she'd loved her husband at first, it had been years since they'd shared a truly happy union.

But it was no time to be mulling over the past. Craig was gone and she'd taken steps to go on with her life.

The throaty, masculine voice snaking down the hall made her snap upright. Nick sauntered toward her. "I guess taking care of five is pretty hard work, huh?"

She hadn't seen much of him since dinner—a boisterous affair with the children all seated at the table—and there hadn't been much chance to talk. He'd eaten heartily and pushed away from the table with a satisfied expression, thrown his carefully ironed linen napkin onto the plate and excused himself.

Now, Tracy saw he'd showered and changed into clean jeans and a blue chambray shirt. A plain leather belt was strapped around his lean hips. She wanted to ask where his flashy buckle was, but didn't dare. It might indicate that she'd been looking where she ought not to.

"Yes, it's hard work caring for five kids. But it's what I like doing—so I don't mind." She flattened her hands on the oak chair rail behind her, for some reason feeling jittery. In the low light, Nick's half smile appeared faintly derisive.

Without warning he asked, "Want a drink? I usually have a shot or two when the kids go down and the house is quiet." He gestured for her to walk ahead of him down the long curving staircase as if her answer was given. For just a second she was tempted to decline, simply to thwart him.

But the truth was she could use a soothing tot. Never much of a drinker, Tracy nevertheless thought longingly about the velvet warmth of brandy on her tongue and nodded.

She moved ahead, conscious of Nick's dark eyes on her back. He made her uncomfortable, all right, she admitted silently. Especially when he looked her over with the eye of an expert horseman contemplating the purchase of a prize mare. Amused with the image, Tracy hoped he found her confirmation sound.

Then, she wondered why she should even care.

They descended together, Nick silent and brooding, Tracy, nervous, but with a small, secret smile lending mystery to her features. Downstairs, they had the family room to themselves, Aunt Millie and David having retired early. At the wet bar, Nick turned his back. He poured himself a drink first, then, without bothering to face her, asked over his shoulder what she wanted.

"Brandy," she said, taking the opportunity to assess the wiry length of his body. Hatless now, Nick's teak hair was tousled, and Tracy suspected there wasn't a comb manufactured yet that could tame it. His chambray shirt stretched taut over his lean back; she could easily see the ridged muscles beneath and felt an unfamiliar softening in the region of her stomach.

Heartburn, probably.

The scarred leather belt fit his hips like a glove, and his firm buttocks and strong thighs were outlined under the faded jeans. Pointed toe snakeskin boots formed to his feet and Tracy wondered wryly if he ever took them off.

"Like what you see?"

Tracy's rapt gaze shot upward to Nick's cynical face. "What?"

He grimaced, thrusting a crystal balloon goblet half-filled with amber liquid into her hands. "I've been looked over by buckle bunnies from the muddy Mississippi to New York, from Billings, Montana to Phoenix, Arizona. I know a woman on the make when I see one." He tossed back a hefty swallow of Scotch.

"On, no. I'm not...I wasn't..." She let her words trail off. Nick had one hand propped on his hips, his glass held negligently in the other. It was his expression of disbelieving cynicism that stopped her.

Suddenly she was angry. She felt the heat rise in her cheeks and gritted her teeth. "I'm here to take care of the kids. Kyle and Kitty and my own. That's all. I guess I can look you over if I feel like it." She tilted her chin defiantly. "That is, unless you don't want me to. In that case I'll try to keep my eyes on the walls and the chairs and anything but you. It could get kind of awkward, though, when we speak to each other. You, looking at me, talking to me, and me, looking at the wallpaper."

Surprising her, Nick threw his head back and laughed, the hearty sound ringing through the room. She hadn't expected him to appreciate her sarcasm. If anyone had asked her earlier, she would have bet he never laughed at all.

"I didn't say I didn't like you checking me over," he said, draining his glass and turning back for a refill.

"God, what does it take to get so cynical?" she asked, but she already knew the answer. Part of it, anyway. Nick was a woman hater. Tracy wondered what his mother had done to make him so bitter. She already knew about Eliza.

"Not much. Just a lot of long years of living—of using and getting used by people." He moved to drop into a kid-leather easy chair and let his speculative gaze slide down her figure. "Where've you been, anyway—so innocentlike? A woman like you—a former wife and a mama to three kids. You've been around, haven't you, honey? What'd your old man do to make you leave him, anyway? Or was it the other way around?"

Close to rage, Tracy clenched the brandy snifter so tightly she feared she might break it. With trembling fingers, she lifted it to her lips and allowed the fiery liquor to ease down her throat. It took an effort of will to speak. "Not that I owe you an explanation, but I didn't leave my 'old man,' nor did he leave me."

A heavy dark brow lifted.

"I'm a widow. We were married eight years when Craig was killed in an accident. If he hadn't died we'd still be married today." It was the truth, she thought painfully. She would probably still be married, although not happily. But the rude, nosy Nicholas Roberts didn't need to know that.

She'd had enough. Rising, Tracy placed her still half-full glass on the coffee table. She was shocked when Nick's strong hand whipped out to clamp around her wrist. A little of the brandy sloshed over the rim. She hadn't heard him rise or seen him move toward her. He was simply there.

"Wait."

Wary, Tracy hesitated. "I'm no masochist, Nick. I know when I'm not liked, even though I'm not completely sure why. If you don't want to be around me I'll do my best to avoid you . . . and keep my kids away from you, too."

She meant it, Nick realized in amazement. He searched her wide hazel eyes for any hint of duplicity and figured himself a good enough judge of character to recognize sincerity when he saw it. He hadn't meant to be so darned rude, he told himself, rubbing at his jaw where an itchy five-o'clock beard shadowed his face. He'd just seen so many like her—this Tracy Wilborough.

Releasing her hand, he said, "Look, I don't want you going out of your way avoiding me. It'd be damned awkward, anyhow. As for the kids, I already like them and they like me. I promised your older two this afternoon that I'd teach them to ride."

Tracy's eyes widened. "You did? Whatever for?"

He didn't like the astonished look spreading over her pretty face. It made him feel mean spirited and small. It irritated him that she couldn't believe he was capable of kindness, at least to children. Yet, if he was honest, he knew she had reason.

"Y'all are livin' on a ranch now, honey. You've got to learn to ride," he drawled.

"I know how to ride."

He grinned. "Good. Then I won't have to teach you, too."

With a frown, Tracy considered him. She didn't return his smile, not that he expected her to. He'd been rude at first and now, for some reason, was turning on the charm.

Confused by his own behavior, Nick moved in quick strides to the bar, tossing a few ice cubes into his glass. If *he* was confused, he couldn't begin to wonder what she must be thinking. He only knew he would rather have her looking at him with that slow interested gleam in her eye than the worried expression she now wore.

She appeared to have come to a decision. She folded her hands in front of her, still standing as if contemplating flight. "That's very nice of you, Nick, but I'm sure with all your duties here at the ranch you won't have time for—"

"I said I'd teach them, dammit. Woman, don't you listen?" At her deepening frown, he hurried to temper his words. "You're right that I won't have much time in another month or so. When fall roundup starts we're all pretty busy. But before that and after it, I will. Okay?"

But the recalcitrant woman was shaking her head like a cutting horse that didn't want to be saddled. She wasn't taking any chances. "Thank you. But I don't think so." She turned to leave.

"Tracy."

At the mention of her name, he saw her whirl toward him. It was the first time he'd used it, and it felt right. It was a comfortable name. Good and practical and pretty. Like her.

"Yes?"

He hesitated. It wasn't right and proper—him being mean to her before. He picked at a callous on his thumb, wondering how to explain without giving himself away. At a loss, he jerked around to face the bar. "Aw, the hell with it. You teach 'em."

He felt rather than saw her expression tighten. Then she exited the room, leaving him alone with his dark thoughts. He figured he wasn't decent company for anybody, much less for a spirited, golden-haired beauty like Tracy.

Morosely, Nick stared into his glass. He was a loner, that was all. He'd come into the world that way, and that's the way he would go out. And in between he'd make do.

He was a loner, dammit.

It was the way things were supposed to be—the way he liked them. There wasn't anybody to worry about or care for or tell him what to do.

When he needed a woman he found temporary company with one of the buckle bunnies, where there were no strangling ties to keep him shackled and unhappy.

On the sofa Nick leaned his head back and let his legs jut out. Closing his eyes, he recalled the way Tracy had inspected him—as if she liked what she saw and was trying, somehow, to see beneath his tough exterior.

Nick let out a short, mirthless laugh. She couldn't know there *was* nothing else. Nothing except bitterness and anger and a deep, abiding sense of betrayal. Nick hoped Tracy hadn't already set her mind on lassoing him. He wasn't the settling kind. No, David would suit her more—steady, reliable, serious David. Yes, David was a damn sight more suitable, Nick thought. Only, he was still in love with his deserting wife.

Women!

He would never let one wind her tentacles around him—he'd damn well guarantee it! Because if Nicholas Roberts knew anything it was this—he was a loner and he'd damn well stay that way!

Morning brought with it bright sunshine, heat and an eager Tracy, looking forward to getting to know Kyle and Kitty and exploring the ranch. After a breakfast of steaming oatmeal and buttered toast, Tracy put down her spoon and wiped Kitty's face free of jam. The two of them were alone at the table since the other children had already eaten. She assumed the men had left earlier for work.

Nick came clumping into the house, his boots loud on the hardwood flooring. He hesitated when he saw her. With both hands on his hips, dusty hat pulled low over his forehead, assessing eyes cool, he was the picture of aggression. "We get up before the sun, here, *Miss California*."

Tracy gritted her teeth. She knew exactly what he meant by the title. That she was used to an easy life filled with days spent suntanning on the beach and partying Hollywood-style and doing very little work.

She tried not to rise to the bait, failing miserably. She rounded her eyes with the innocent air of a child. "Oh, my goodness. Perhaps I ought to borrow an alarm clock. I'd thought my usual wake-up time of five-thirty would suffice."

"Five-thir—you're up that early every day?" Nick asked, appearing gratifingly surprised.

"Toby wakes early, and he needs to be changed and dressed and he's always starving. He's having a nap now. And then I have to see about breakfast for Brady and Dan. They need supervision with their morning chores— you know, cleaning their room, laundry—that sort of thing." She went on in the same breezy voice, "And now I've got Kitty and Kyle to care for. I noticed Kitty likes to eat right away when she wakes up, too. Gosh, I guess you're right. Five-thirty really *is* too late."

Nick cleared his throat. "Five-thirty's all right, I guess." He moved off and Tracy watched his retreating back with triumph. The man had a lot of nerve, especially since she'd been hired by David.

Last night after leaving him in the family room to drink alone, she'd vowed to speak to him only when spoken to. She hadn't liked the restless tension she'd experienced when he gripped her wrist and she had decided to stay out of his way.

But when he strode into the house just now, challenging her, she just couldn't keep still. The gall!

"Wanna get down!" Kitty demanded, wriggling in her chair. Tracy took a paper napkin and cleaned the oatmeal from between the little girl's fingers and set her on the floor.

Tracy stood smoothed her palms over her old jeans, flattening out creases. She tucked a bit of hair behind her ear that had escaped her long French braid. Then she did the same for Kitty's tiny braid.

"Let's go thank Aunt Millie for such good food," Tracy suggested, leading Kitty by the hand to the saloon doors. Just then a yawning Toby came down the curving staircase, rubbing his eyes. His chubby hands clung to the wooden handrail as he descended, putting one foot on each lower stair before joining it with the other.

A rush of love rose up so strong Tracy felt tears forming behind her lids. How she loved her boys. And how fortunate she was to be able to earn a living and stay with Toby during his formative years. She wouldn't have to fret over paying electric bills or fixing broken appliances or making the rent. All that was taken care of now. She had only to be conscientious in caring for the children. This job was a godsend!

Kitty gave a cry of delight and sped over to Toby to take his hand and swing it between their bodies.

"Toady!" she cried. An angelic grin spread over her face.

"No," he said.

"Now, Toby, say good morning to Kitty. She's going to be your new friend, remember?" Tracy sat on the second stair, curving an arm around both children.

"No!" Toby insisted, wrapping strangling arms about her neck.

Tracy sighed. Kitty's blue eyes looked at her expectantly. She'd better get them busy, Tracy thought. They'd be playing together before they knew it. At least she didn't have to worry about Brady and Dan for a while. Kyle had promised to show them the stables and livestock and even the new litter of kittens in the barn. They'd been sternly admonished by Tracy to stay out of the ranchhands' way and keep out of trouble. She hoped they'd taken her warning to heart.

In a small fenced yard leading off the kitchen, Tracy found child-sized furniture and toys. She was relieved there would be somewhere for the two youngest to play safely without constant supervision. There she discovered an old set of Kyle's finger paints, a roll of butcher paper and plastic aprons and set the two young children to work in the shade.

"See, Kitty? You mush your hands in the bowl of paint like this, then rub it all over the paper. Good, Toby. I like that bright red design. What is it? The Blob?"

"Da blob," he repeated happily, getting paint in his hair.

"Goodness sakes!" Millie exclaimed from the kitchen door. "I never!" She stepped out, bending over to peer at the mess. Straightening, she smiled at Tracy. "I don't believe Kitty's ever painted before. Sure looks fun."

"Never painted?" Tracy asked in amazement. "She's three years old. Why not?"

Millie thrust her hands into her calico apron's pockets. "Eliza didn't like the fuss."

"See what I do!" Kitty said with a huge grin. She proudly held her paper up to Millie while the paint dripped down.

"Sweetheart, that's just wonderful," Millie praised. "And yours is so good too, Toby."

Toby held up his own creation. "Da blob," he told her solemnly.

She nodded, asking, "How about some of my snicker doodles and milk?"

"Cookies, cookies!" chorused both children.

"Millie!" Tracy exclaimed. "It's eight o'clock in the morning. You can't give them cookies now."

Suitably chagrined, Millie pursed her lips. "After lunch, then?"

"Yes, that'll be fine." She faced a crestfallen Toby and Kitty. "After lunch—one each."

"Only one?" Millie looked shocked.

"Millie."

"All right, all right." She turned back to the kitchen mumbling, "A body'd think a couple of cookies'd kill you." But at the door she smiled at Tracy.

A half an hour later, the project cleaned up and most of the paint washed from the children's hair, Tracy laid the artwork out to dry and decided she would walk about the ranch a bit and take the children with her. She headed toward the long bank of stables, hoping to see what kind of horseflesh the Roberts clan considered quality.

But the first thing she did was run into Nick.

In a small paddock behind the stables she came upon him and the three boys. Although she knew Nick must be aware of her presence, he ignored her. A buckskin horse stood inside a split-rail fence. The gelding was bridled but had only a soft saddle pad cinched to his back.

Tracy came up short, her grip around both Toby's and Kitty's tiny hands tightening. Nick was explaining the intricacies of horseback riding, obviously intending to set Brady aboard the horse. Inwardly bristling, she had a sudden urge to leap forward and snatch Brady away.

"...The first thing I'm gonna do is give you a leg up—"

"Gosh, Nick, what's a leg up?" Brady interrupted.

"What's a leg up?" Dan echoed.

"A yeghup," repeated Toby.

Kyle snickered behind a hand and even Kitty giggled.

But Nick asked patiently, "How do you suppose you're going to get on this big ol' buckskin to ride him, boy?"

Brady, who'd never been this close to a horse in his whole eight years, studied a dirty fingernail. Then, in a hopeful voice, he offered, "A ladder?"

When Kyle laughed openly, Nick glared at him. He turned back to Brady. "No, boy. A horse won't stand still for a ladder. See how I lace my fingers together like this? Now you put your foot there and throw your other leg across the animal's back. Got it?"

Poor Brady's eyes widened even more—so much so that Tracy could see white around the entire circumference of his irises. Her jaw clenched at his obvious apprehension. Why was Nick pushing her son this way? He ought to let Brady get used to the horse—maybe lead him around the corral for a while or simply watch the more experienced, older Kyle for a day or so.

Before she could speak, she heard Brady say, "Uh, yes sir," put his shaking foot in the mock stirrup of Nick's hands and climb onto the horse's back. Nick thrust the leather reins into Brady's hands. The buckskin immediately set off at a fast walk.

Drawn forward by trepidation, Tracy admonished the two youngest to stay far back from the fence, then leaned her elbows on the second rail.

Nick yelled instructions to the boy, who had his hands full trying to control the horse. When Brady finally understood the simple technique of holding the reins in one fist and pulling the leather straps to the side in which he wished to go, he glanced back at Nick, his face flushed and grinning with pride.

Nick fell silent, propping one booted heel behind him on the bottom rail of the corral. With a calloused thumb he nudged his hat until it sat far back on his head. He didn't look at Tracy when he said, "Your boy's got a good seat. He's gonna be a natural." He watched as Brady leaned forward to pat the buckskin's shining coat. "Seems to have affection for the horse, too. That's important."

"I thought you weren't going to teach them to ride." Tracy said, afraid to take her eyes off Brady.

She felt his sideways glance. "I promised the boys I would."

"Yes, but last night—"

"I always keep my promises."

Tracy looked at him, again feeling that jolt of attraction when their gazes collided. Somehow he engendered in her a profound awareness of her own femininity. When he studied her, she felt soft and womanly and totally vulnerable.

With an effort, she tore her gaze away. She didn't like it when he failed to make the same effort to break the bond. He kept his gaze on her profile—she could feel the force and heat and utter danger his scrutiny produced.

He made her feel a little breathless, unsure and lightheaded. With a nervous gesture, she ran stiff fingers down her braid.

The loud wail and soft thud coming from across the ring jerked both their heads around in time to see Brady sprawled in the hard-packed dirt. The boy lay exactly between the solid hooves of the big buckskin.

Chapter Three

"Son!" Tracy scrambled through the bars and rushed across the arena as fast as her terrified legs could go. Her heart in her throat, she reached the crying boy. She knelt beside him. "Brady! Oh, my God!"

The horse had calmly picked his way over the boy and began moving toward a small clump of weeds growing at one end of the ring.

"Get up, boy, you're all right," Nick said heartlessly, hauling him up. "Go on over there and fetch your horse. The only thing to do is get back on."

"Nick!" Tracy exclaimed, hugging Brady close like a mother bear whose cubs were threatened by a mountain lion. "I can't believe you're so callous. He's hurt, for God's sake. Can't you see it?"

"Nah," Nick said. "The horse was at a walk. Brady's not hurt, just a little shook up. We all take a spill now and then."

"Maybe you do!" she rounded on him. "Of course *you* don't think it's serious—a man who makes his living falling off horses!"

"Begging your pardon, ma'am." His gaze abruptly hardened. "I make my living staying *on* horses."

"Whatever," she threw back. "It's all your fault. Brady wasn't ready to leap on any old horse's back. He needs thorough instruction—a slow introduction to riding. Not a sink or swim sort of lesson."

Brady had stopped crying and merely mewled softly.

Nick's voice rose a bit. "The only way to learn to ride a horse is to ride him. What'd you want me to do? Give him a manual?"

Tracy led her son back toward the railing and helped him through. Under her breath she muttered, "Oh, I don't know why I allowed you to go through with this, anyway. I ought to just do it myself."

"I said I'd teach these boys to ride, and I will!" Nick thundered. He followed her through the railing and touched her elbow. "Understand?"

She shook him off. "No, I don't—"

"Mom it's okay." It was Brady whispering at her side.

Surprised, Tracy glanced down. "Honey, I don't think—"

"I can do it, I know I can. It's my fault I fell off. I think I leaned too far forward, patting Jackson's neck." Brady kicked at the ground, sending up a miniature dustcloud. "I guess I wasn't paying attention." He faced Nick. "Give me another chance, okay?" He snuck a glance at Kyle, who was watching with great interest. "Please, Nick?"

"Sure, son. Go get the horse and lead him over here."

Meeting Nick's eyes, Tracy expected to see triumph and was startled when his expression was unexpectedly neutral. She'd figured him to be the type to lord it over another when he'd won a point. But he hadn't.

Nick had shown a surprising graciousness, for which she was grateful. Brady apparently felt he had to prove himself before Kyle and Nick—his young masculine ego already showing a healthy desire to appear capable in front of other males. Tracy knew she could never humiliate him by forcing the issue, even for his own good. Still, she couldn't help glowering a last time at Nick.

Brady climbed back onto the buckskin and finished the lesson, this time taking care to pay close attention to Nick's instructions. Next, it was Dan's turn. Tracy bit her lip but remained silent. The younger boy was even more awkward, although he managed to stay on the saddle pad.

When Nick suggested putting Toby atop, Tracy put her foot down. She gathered Toby and Kitty close and hightailed it for the house before Nick could argue. She resolved to allow Nick to continue the lessons if he wanted, but she would no longer watch. It was possible she was making the boys nervous. Deep down, she realized he was careful—not letting Brady and Dan, with their newly-found confidence, coax the horse into a faster gait as they each had begged him to.

Thus, she was feeling an unaccustomed acceptance toward Nick that evening.

She was soon to regret it.

As usual Millie had rustled up a delicious meal—thick slabs of roast beef, fluffy mashed potatoes and fresh green beans. Afterward, the kids were all sacked out on the living room floor in front of the television. David was reading a book on cattle-embryo transplanting and Millie was giving the dining table a last wipe.

Tracy stepped onto the veranda to admire the striking sunset forming on the horizon. Breathing deeply, she took in the clean air. She leaned against a post at the edge of the porch. Deep russet, blending into golden amber, streaked across the unending sky. She smiled. Yes, she'd done the right thing, coming to Montana. This land was peaceful... lulling... just what she wanted and needed.

From childhood, she'd cherished memories of life on a ranch. She wanted her boys to know the old-fashioned definition of work and reward. She wanted them to hold dear the values she'd been taught—to be kind to others, work hard, love the land. They would find it here. Everything was perfect.

Then Nick joined her.

He leaned a shoulder against the other post, only a few feet away. Snapping open his lighter, he nodded at her once, then inhaled until the end of his cigarette glowed in the fading dusk. His features were thrown into relief in the uncertain light. His lean cheeks and jutting nose were weathered and remote. But his eyes weren't. When he turned to her she fancied his dark eyes gleamed. For her.

Tracy shook herself, irritated at the ridiculous notion.

He said, "You were upset today."

"I'm over it now." She remembered feeling grateful to Nick earlier and kept her tones even. Shifting her weight, she turned now-unseeing eyes toward the sunset. "It was a shock, that's all, when Brady fell like that."

"I think it'd be a good idea if you didn't hang around while I'm teaching the boys."

Completely forgetting her resolution to do that very thing, she straightened, demanding, "Why?"

He shrugged, flicking an ash. "They don't need an audience."

"I'm not an audience. I'm their mother!"

"Let's just say *I* don't need an audience."

"So that's it!"

"Yeah, that's it. If I'm gonna teach these boys right I can't have a softhearted, interfering mama sticking her two cents in where it isn't wanted."

Tracy blinked. Some other, calmer part of her was able to stand back and admire the man's sheer arrogance and nerve. Never had she met anyone with such unshakable self-confidence.

But the main part of her—the surface part that wasn't so calm—marshalled her most cutting retort. How could she have felt even a momentary softening or, God forbid, any *true* admiration for him? The idea was incredible. She was about to bestow a piece of her mind on Nick when Kitty's sweet voice called out.

It diverted her, quieting the building anger. Why was she wasting emotion on him, anyway?

Tracy turned to leave, putting one hand on the door jamb. There, she paused. "You're a maverick, aren't you, Nick? You don't bother with such silly conventions as attempting to be *nice* or *accommodating* or even *courteous*. Oh, no. Not you."

"I'll tell you one thing, *Miss California*. I am different from other men in one way. I'm sure as hell not getting suckered into believing myths about women."

"What myths?"

Nick ground the butt of his cigarette in an ashtray with a savage twist of his hand. "That some of you are special. Which damn well isn't so. You're all alike—you women. You all run off when things get sticky. Like now. Trouble is, you aren't *man* enough to stand here and talk this out."

"I'm not running off. Kitty's calling me." She glared at him frostily.

"Yes, you are. And when the going on this ranch gets rough, you'll take off, too."

Staring at him, Tracy wondered who they were really discussing. Millie had said his mother was "not exactly a saint." What had she done to so embitter Nick? Perhaps she'd abandoned Nick and David as boys. Certainly Eliza had left David, and Tracy knew Nick was furious about that. But hadn't there been other, kinder, faithful women in his life? Curiosity about Nick's romantic relationships nibbled at the edges of her mind. Was every one of them a disaster?

It didn't matter. She wasn't responsible for the behavior of two women she'd never met—or for any others who may have broken his heart. She didn't have to take the abuse Nick obviously needed to vent.

Gathering dignity, she drew herself up. "Sorry to disappoint you, but I won't 'take off.' I love it here. I consider this home, now. My only problem is *you*." With that she strode away to find Kitty.

One week later she and Nick were still sidling around each other like edgy polecats. Tracy knew his gaze followed her—studying, weighing her worth, challenging. She didn't know exactly what he thought because he said little.

And because of his scrutiny and few words, she found herself keeping a sort of watch over him, too. It seemed that at all times she knew where he was in a room, and even in which part of the ranch he would be working that day. She noticed his clothing—always jeans and a Western shirt topped by his hat. Sometimes he'd roll his sleeves up over his corded forearms, revealing the twisting scar. She wanted to ask about it, but didn't dare.

Sometimes he would come in for lunch after repairing fencing or equipment, dusty and sweaty. Since she often helped Millie with the cooking, she would be there when he arrived. Unbuttoning his shirt, he'd soap his face and hands at the cold-water faucet outside the kitchen door. As he leaned over the small sink, Tracy tried not to let her eyes wander down the broad expanse of tanned chest to where his skin, unavailable to the sun, was lighter. Dark curling hair furrowed down in a neat triangle to disappear into his jeans, and Tracy tried not to notice that, either.

And because of her awareness, she noticed that sometimes, for a day or so, Nick disappeared.

Casually, she tried asking Millie, who exhibited an uncharacteristic nonchalance about Nick's whereabouts. Mentioning his absence to the boys, by way of asking about their riding lessons, revealed they didn't know where he escaped to, either. There seemed to be no explanation. It was curious, Tracy thought. Odd.

Nick had been gone all the day before and that morning when Tracy had settled the two toddlers down for an afternoon nap. Feeling lazy in the August heat, she ambled through the house, telling Millie she was going to visit the horses. Inside the cool barn, Tracy produced a small apple for Jackson, the placid buckskin on whom her boys were learning to ride. The horse leaned eagerly over the stall to snatch the prize from her hand. She patted his neck and thought about asking David if she could take him out to ride.

Remembering the simple rope hackamore she'd used on the shetland pony she owned as a child, Tracy wandered into the tack room to examine the dozens of saddles, kept in neat order on heavy boards that jutted from the wall. Odors of saddle soap and linament and hay brought back the scents of her childhood. And memories. Good ones. Fingering a finely braided, seasoned leather bridle, Tracy whirled in surprise at the sound of Nick's voice.

"You like that bridle?" Nick stood in the doorway, filling it.

"This?" Tracy dropped her hand as if burned. "Uh, yes. It's terrific workmanship. I've never seen such a beautiful piece of tack."

Nick nodded in satisfaction. "I made it." He crossed the room with the loose-jointed, athletic gait she was beginning to think of as uniquely his.

"Did you? I'd like to be able to do work like this. Does it take a lot of practice?"

"Some." He ran careful fingers over the bridle.

"Don't worry." She was suddenly defensive, crossing her arms over her breasts. "I wasn't going to ask you to teach me." Why did he have to stand so close? Where had he been yesterday and today? Why did she feel so skittish around him?

"That's good."

Tracy took refuge in sarcasm. "A man of few words, aren't you? I won't waste any more of your time. I'll leave."

"Where are you going?"

She paused, throwing over her shoulder, "I don't know. Just out of your way."

"Don't go."

His command stopped her. She faced him slowly, aware of a subtle change in the atmosphere between them. He was close. So close that she had only to lean forward a bit to fall into his embrace. She caught his clean, soapy scent. Normally he kept his dark hair brushed back, under the hat. But today, a bit of the unruly stuff fell over his forehead; she resisted a crazy urge to reach up and smooth it back. Instead, she asked, "Why shouldn't I go?"

"I want you to stay. We could talk." His eyes kept her prisoner. She watched in fascination as he swallowed thickly. Moving his arm up, he casually placed one hand against the wall beside her face—cutting off her escape.

That one, innocuous gesture alarmed her more than anything else he could have done. Anything except kissing her.

Now where had that wild idea come from, Wilborough?

But of course he didn't kiss her, or even move closer. He simply asked her a few questions about the boys. Innocent questions like how they felt about living on a ranch—how they were getting along with Kyle and Kitty. Within moments Tracy felt herself relaxing a bit. Nick's quiet interest lulled her.

A short silence fell between them, then lengthened while they studied each other until Tracy began to wonder if he was indeed thinking of kissing her. Especially when she realized with a jolt that he was looking at her mouth.

She had no more time to wonder because Nick's hand dropped to her shoulder, this time with no pretense of being casual. His low voice hummed over her, tempting her. "Well. I've about run out of talk. Maybe we could think of something else to do. Got any ideas?"

Under her crossed arms, Tracy felt her breasts grow heavy and full. Her knees, rigidly locked with tension minutes ago, now felt languid and rubbery—like they wanted someone else to support them. Like a man.

She stared at him, almost unable to think. She felt hypnotized by his eyes, blazing into hers with sexual promise. "N-no. I don't have any other ideas."

Flashing a grin, Nick moved his hand to the juncture of her neck and shoulder. His long fingers touched the collar of her blouse and then her throat. "That's too bad, honey, 'cause I've got plenty of 'em."

"Plenty of what?" she replied stupidly. For the life of her, she couldn't remember what they were talking about. The slightly raspy feel of Nick's calloused fingers on her sensitive skin was crowding out all other thoughts.

His smile was tender now, and knowing. Tracy couldn't take her eyes off his face. She hadn't known the tough-as-nails man had a tender atom in his body.

On a growling whisper, he said, "We were talking about other ideas, honey. But the ones in my mind are kind of off-limits. I'm having thoughts that aren't sensible. Such as touching and liking the touching so much it leads to more. I'm thinking of soft, bare shoulders," he whispered, tracing a lazy circle over her flesh with his thumb, "and sweet lips." His heated gaze on her mouth incited a turmoil of unpardonable sensuality in her lower abdomen. With his nearness, the turmoil grew and spread, further weakening her knees and her resolve. "I'm thinking that you'd best skedaddle out of this barn, honey, before we're both sorry."

Tracy swallowed hard. By inches, she edged back until his hand fell away. "Y-yes. We'd best...I'll just...well, bye." With that she turned tail and ran as if a whole herd of stampeding cattle were hard on her heels.

Outside, after running the gamut of the long bank of stalls, she paused for breath and sanity, leaning over to press shaking hands to her thighs. What had she been doing—exchanging innuendoes with the disreputable, rude, careless brother of her employer? Had she been that lonely? she asked herself in remorse. Her anger transferred to him.

"Damn that cowboy!" she muttered. From his point of view he was just trifling with the resident nanny. It meant nothing. He must have had many such flirtations. He'd probably already forgotten.

But from her end, things were more serious. She'd never made a habit of flirting with Cassanova-types, about whom she ought to know better. He'd shaken her because she hadn't known, or at least she'd denied knowing that she was incredibly, vibrantly attracted to him.

Several days later nothing had changed.

But Tracy discovered that she could avoid him, and during the ensuing days, she did with scrupulous care. She soon became quite adept at it. To her relief, and not at all to her dismay she reassured herself for the tenth time, he didn't pursue her.

In the middle of the week, however, she could no longer remain silent. That morning she'd noticed Nick's high spirits when he came in for lunch and she'd overheard him telling David about the new two-year-old colt he was considering for purchase that would be arriving that day. The horse, she gathered, would mark the beginning of a new branch for the cattle enterprise—Roberts Racing Quarterhorses.

Always a horse lover, Tracy heard the commotion out front and knew the colt had arrived. She shooed the three older boys, with whom she was playing gin rummy, outside. They ran yelling in excitement up to the big blue-striped trailer. Even Tracy, not well versed in horse breeding, recognized the distinctive yellow thunderbolt on the trailer as belonging to the Cordola family—a

Kentucky breeding farm highly respected in racing circles.

Out front, rose bushes flanked the long verandah and a circular driveway had been built to allow plenty of vehicles to maneuver. A tall oak shaded the house, somewhat set back from the drive, and from under its cool branches Tracy observed.

Nick was there, his pleasure evident in his wide smile. He was talking with the driver and another man. Wiry and in his forties, the man had thinning hair and a suede vest over his shirt. He represented the Cordolas. Nick gave only a cursory glance at the black quarter horse the driver was backing out of the trailer. But Tracy was awed. She'd never been this close to such a magnificent animal.

With some trouble, the driver got the horse out. High-spirited, the colt's finely-arched neck tossed proudly. He sidestepped, dancing, while the driver hung on to his hackamore. Tracy took in the ebony-sleek coat and sighed. The horse was beautiful.

Can't Slow Down, as she heard the driver call the horse, half reared when he felt his hooves touch the loose gravel. The driver murmured to him, patting the velvety muzzle. Nick was so attentive to the Cordola representative he didn't bother turning to watch. He was really taken with the whole situation, Tracy marveled. She heard him enthusiastically cataloging the sterling lineage of the colt with the other man. But he wasn't really looking at the horse.

"Wow!" Kyle said, his hands thrust into his front pockets. "That's an *awesome* horse!"

"Yeah," agreed Brady, eager to sound knowledgeable. "He's got a... a real long neck."

Kyle punched him in the arm. "Ya don't need a long neck to run fast, Brady," he chided.

"Long ne—" Dan halted his usual echo in the middle when he realized that it was wrong. "Long, ah, legs," he amended.

"Right," Kyle agreed. "A good racehorse has gotta have long legs. And he's got 'em."

Dan beamed. Brady just looked sheepish.

That's when Tracy saw them. Straight pasterns. Well, not exactly straight, she amended, only subtly so. She might never have noticed if the boy's comments hadn't induced her to stare at the colt's legs. For a racehorse— or one meant to sire champions—it was a serious flaw. The pasterns, the bones that ran along the front of a horse's legs, had to be angled for speed. And Can't Slow Down's pasterns wouldn't pass the standards of Nick's eagle eye.

She stood well back, keeping the boys away from the spirited colt and waited for Nick to discover the flaw. He talked for a few more minutes to the Cordola representative, then turned to glide a quick hand down the colt's back. With a grin, he gave the horse a satisfied whack on the rump.

"I like him," she heard Nick inform the man. "He just might make a fine stallion for my racing stable." Nick looked down at the clipboard of papers in his hand and started reading the fine print. The other man let out a long breath as if relieved.

Puzzled, Tracy again studied the horse. She put up a hand to shade her eyes from the August sun shining on the coal-dark coat. Again she came to her original conclusion. The horse was flawed. Her next thought was that Nick hadn't seen it. He couldn't have. He hadn't taken the time to really inspect the animal.

Before she had time to think, she called to Nick. His head jerked up from his reading. He frowned at her from across the drive. "What? I'm busy right now."

"I know, Nick, but I've got to talk with you."

His frown deepened and he flipped the papers flat with an irritated snap. "Can't it wait?"

"No. It can't. Please."

"Mr. Roberts," the representative said, fingering the pockets of his vest. "There are other buyers interested in the horse. We're on a schedule. If you don't mind?"

"This'll just take a second." Nick stalked across the drive, boots crunching loud on the gravel, his expression warning her with a this-had-better-be-good scowl.

Tracy chewed the inside of her lip. Sudden indecision gripped her. Why had she imagined she knew more about horses than a Montana rancher? Why had she opened her big mouth?

He stood there, all impatient features and demanding tone. "Well?"

She averted her eyes. "Ah, I didn't mean to interrupt. It's just that ... well ..."

"Spit it out, Tracy. The man's in a hurry."

Behind her back she twisted her fingers together. "Um ..." She mumbled the problem under her breath.

"I can't hear you, woman. Speak up!"

"Don't yell at me. I thought you should know," she swallowed, then whispered urgently, "the horse has straight pasterns."

His eyes hard and brittle as brown glass, Nick studied her for a long moment. Then he swung around to view the colt. He approached the stamping horse and stopped, leaning over to guide knowing fingers along the legs. Slowly, he rose, muttering, "I'll be damned."

"Mr. Roberts, if we may conclude our transaction?" the horse dealer pressed. His thumbs were thrust into his vest pockets and his fingers drummed impatiently on his ribs.

Nick faced him. "Well, sir, looks like you don't have a sale after all."

"Beg your pardon?" The fingers stopped drumming.

"Your colt isn't quite to my liking. When I'm planning to spend that much on a horse I want him perfect. He isn't. But thanks for stopping by. Say hello to Randy Cordola when you get a chance." With that, Nick pulled his hat low over his eyes and strode toward the house.

The man raised a hand with a halfhearted protest, but when he saw Nick wasn't going to stop, he shrugged and motioned for the driver to lead the colt back into the trailer.

Kyle, Brady and Dan chased after their idol, peppering him with questions. Wasn't he gonna buy the horse? Why was that driver loading him back in? Why were they taking him away?

Tracy followed, uncertain, into the cool foyer. She didn't know how the proud man would take her interference. Nick was in the family room. He answered the boys' questions, then suggested they go check on the new kittens in the main barn. Since it was almost time to get Toby and Kitty up from their naps, she placed one foot on the bottom stair, but stopped when Nick called her name.

"Yes?" she said, not turning around. She didn't think it a good idea, their being alone. Not after what had happened in the tack room.

"Come here."

Slowly Tracy approached, stopping several feet shy of the laconic man. He waited until she raised her eyes to his.

"You were right. Those pasterns weren't sound and his legs were light, too. I almost made a costly mistake. The horse had been described to me by Randy Cordola over the phone as a fine colt—and I figured I'd take the man on his word." Nick shrugged. "No wonder they were selling him off instead of racing him. I should've examined him closer. Guess I was just too darn excited about finally starting my racing stable."

"It's understandable," Tracy murmured.

"No, it's not," he returned harshly. When Tracy winced, he half turned away, fists clenched. "How could I have been so damned stupid?" Visibly gathering poise, he made an effort to calm down. "Anyway, thanks." His steady gaze held hers, and she thought she detected a hint of admiration in their brown depths. "I didn't realize you knew anything about horses. Where did you grow up?"

"A small ranch in California."

"Ah."

"Mount Shasta. I've always hated city life—the crowds, the noise, the pollution. For a long time I've wanted to get back to the country. That's why I applied for the job here."

"Didn't your husband like the country?"

"Craig? No, he was a city boy through and through. He couldn't even stand visiting my parents. Every time we'd go to the ranch, he'd sneeze from the hay and complain about the lack of social life." She shrugged, not really condemning Craig. During her marriage she'd accepted his preference for the city.

So she was surprised when Nick's eyes flared in anger. "That was pretty selfish of the man—to make you live where you didn't want to. Why'd you do it?"

"He was my husband," she answered, as if that explained it all. She didn't really want to go into details of her sometimes unhappy life with Craig. Nick didn't need to know Craig had been adamant and unbending. She turned to go.

"Tracy." Nick reached out and put a hand on her arm. Through the soft cotton of her blouse she felt the warm strength of his hand. She fought the urge to shiver.

Keeping her head averted, she looked at his hand until he removed it. "Yes?"

He hesitated. "Uh... just thanks."

"Sure," she replied, heading for the stairs and safety.

Chapter Four

After dinner that night Tracy became aware of a new problem. Or maybe it had been there all along, but she'd been too preoccupied to notice. Kyle didn't like her.

They'd eaten together, as usual, and afterward she bade everyone to stay put, hurried through the saloon doors into the kitchen and reappeared with a steaming blackberry pie fresh from the oven.

"Ta-dah!" she announced, flourishing the pie. "Dessert everyone. And Millie's got vanilla-bean ice cream to go with the pie. Who wants a slice?"

The ensuing din as the kids shouted nearly drowned Nick's question. "Who made it?" he asked suspiciously.

"I did," Tracy answered with pride. "Toby and Kitty and I picked the blackberries this afternoon, and it's been baking while we've eaten dinner. Try some. It's good."

Normally Nick ate with gusto. So when he gingerly took a minuscule bite, Tracy grinned. She had absolute confidence in her pie-making skills.

At the end of the table, David laughed. "It's terrific, Tracy. Don't worry about Nick. I'm afraid he's not appreciative of Millie's efforts at pie baking."

"Harumph!" Millie said, scooping a bite into her mouth.

"You're darn straight!" Nick agreed. "Millie can out cook anybody this side of the Mississippi. But when it comes to my favorite berry pie—she couldn't throw one and hit the broad side of a barn!"

"Now, Nicholas, you know I've tried. It's the crust I just can't get right," Millie said.

"You mean that boot leather you put under the pie last time was supposed to be crust?" Nick teased.

"Nick!" David admonished.

"Yum!" Kitty said, purple pie makings covering half her face.

"Sure is good," Brady said, digging in.

"Good," echoed Dan.

Toby didn't say anything, too busy piling gooey berries on top of each other and watching them fall.

That was when Tracy noticed Kyle wasn't eating. He sat staring at the untouched pie before him. "What's the matter, Kyle," she asked. "Don't you like it?"

"It's okay," he muttered, keeping his head down.

"Kyle," she tried again. "How about some ice cream instead?"

"I don't want any."

Tracy met David's eyes over the boy's head. David raised a perplexed brow. "Kyle," he began, "you feeling all right, son?"

"Yeah."

Tracy watched David lift a dismissing shoulder. He stood and helped carry plates to the kitchen. He cast Tracy an It's-nothing-to-worry-about smile. The others finished their pie, but Tracy, cleaning up Toby, eyed Kyle from across the table. She knew an unhappy boy when she saw one.

Before he could escape, Tracy put a staying hand on his shoulder. The others filed into the family room, and she heard the TV set go on.

When they were alone, Tracy motioned for Kyle to take a seat. She perched on the chair next to him. This was her job; seeing to the emotional well-being of her charges. If she couldn't, she was failing her function.

He sat hunched over, staring at his knee where a hole in his pant leg was fraying. A mutinous expression darkened his features.

Tracy drew a breath. "When I was a kid, I used to love blackberry pie. My friends and I would take big baskets out to the berry patches and we'd pick. But for every berry we put in the basket, one disappeared into our mouths. Have you ever picked berries, Kyle?"

"Yeah. When Mom was here." He slouched deeper into the chair.

A bit of sandy hair flopped over his forehead, and Tracy raised a hand to smooth it. But Kyle flinched away.

Trying not to feel rejected, Tracy concentrated on his comment. "Did your mom pick with you?"

"Sometimes."

"Well. Maybe you and I can go down to the berry patch tomorrow. We could pick a whole bunch and I'll make preserves for toast in the morning. Would you like that, Kyle?" Tracy smiled, trying to catch his eye.

Kyle hesitated, then slid off the chair. He thrust both hands into the front pockets of his cords. "No. I don't want to." He started moving away.

"But, Kyle—"

"Are you gonna make me?" he demanded.

"Of course not. I just thought—"

"Why don't you just leave me alone? I don't want you around here. I'm not your kid and you're not my mom!"

"Kyle..." Tracy started, lifting an ineffectual hand. But the boy had raced out, leaving only the gently swinging door in his wake.

Nick stood in the family room with his back to the others, pouring himself an after-dinner brandy. Despite himself, he had to admit that Tracy really knew horses. And she could bake a heck of a blackberry pie, he thought in grudging admiration.

The TV blared out a prime-time cops-and-robbers show, holding the kids enthralled while Kyle and Tracy lingered in the dining room. Toby was totally involved in rolling a toy truck across the carpet and accompanying it with growling engine sounds. Nick grinned. He liked the little guy. Toby always tried to keep up with Dan, who in turn wanted only to be as manly as *his* big brother.

Brady was doing well in his riding lessons, too. He listened to Nick's instructions and listened hard. When he'd fallen from the buckskin during that first lesson, he'd cried, but he'd gotten right back up. Nick liked that. The boy had grit.

All Tracy's brood were fine kids, he allowed. She was a bit soft on them, but that was to be expected, what with no daddy around to lend a firm hand and all. Nick took a long sip of his drink, wanting to feel the satisfying slide of hard liquor down his throat. But though he felt the heat, he felt none of the satisfaction.

It was because of that damn woman.

Every time Tracy Wilborough's image haunted the edges of his mind, he felt frustration. She was good with the kids, helped out in the kitchen and pretty much kept to herself, as a good nanny should. She hadn't caused any trouble, except for sassing him a little. Yet, he couldn't help an unfamiliar chafing when she was around. Like an itch in the middle of his back—an itch he couldn't scratch.

Downing the rest of the brandy without respect for its excellent year, Nick rubbed a stiff shoulder. Impatiently, he kneaded the sore area, his eyes on the television but not really seeing the screen. There was no denying it—he'd wanted to kiss her in the barn last week. It had to be those huge eyes of hers, so wide and clear and vulnerable as she'd studied him, her fingers stroking the fine leather of the bridle he'd fashioned by hand. It had to be her softly curved body, so slender and rounded and feminine that called out to the man in him.

He remembered testing her, dropping a hand to her shoulder and waiting for her to realize his touch wasn't meant to be platonic. Recalling the soft, soft feel of her skin as he'd dragged his thumb along her collarbone, Nick caught a breath; he'd intensely enjoyed the darkening of her wary eyes. He was sure he hadn't imagined the almost imperceptible way she'd leaned toward him. Oh, she'd reacted to him all right. And he'd wanted her.

It had been best for all that she'd run when she did.

Startling Nick out of his musings, Kyle burst into the room, fists thrust into the front pockets of his jeans, and flopped onto a chair. Scowling into his empty glass, Nick ordered his rapidly heating body to cool. He hadn't realized how merely the image of Tracy could set his jaw tight, his hands fisting, the area below his belt buckle heavy and wanting....

Tracy entered the room and his scowl deepened. Her hazel eyes flashed over him and came to rest on Kyle an instant before he discerned in them a hint of pain. Something was wrong between the new nanny and David's oldest...and Nick wanted nothing more than to stay uninvolved. So what if she knew horses—had in fact saved him a considerable amount of money—and was competent at her work? It was her duty wasn't it, her job?

Muttering an oath, Nick set his glass on the bar and stalked from the room. He didn't want to feel admiration for her. Or desire. Or anything. Those feelings stirred in him emotions he thought long dead. At the foot of the stairs Nick rested a fist on the oak railing. Head bent, he felt his lips thin in remembered agony. In his life women hadn't played straight. His mother hadn't.

He'd known. Even at the tender ages of eight and ten and twelve, he'd known that his mother's licentious habits were slowly killing his father. Neither shouting matches nor fury nor pleading changed things, and Garrison Roberts had run out of ways to try to stop her. He'd found solace only in bottle after bottle of mind-numbing Scotch.

Nick's jaw ached with tension as he remembered. At the top of this very bannister he'd peered, late one night when he was thirteen. The house was mostly dark, lit only by half-burned candles in a wall sconce. Sleepy and wanting a glass of water, he'd paused in the hallway, hearing low voices. Curious, he'd moved to the bannister, rubbing tired eyes, to glance down.

Garrison had been snoring off his Scotch on the family room sofa, waiting for his wife to come home.

But there in the foyer, his mother was oblivious to anything but the ardent embrace of a neighboring rancher, his father's friend. They were kissing—hands groping over each other's clothing. On a gasp of shock, young Nick recoiled into the shadows to slink into his bedroom.

At an age when dawning sexuality was making itself known, Nick had realized the depth of her betrayal. But back then he'd been too young... too young to help his heartbroken father. Too inexperienced to act. And so he'd held it in, this furious resentment, this distrust.

Over the years the women he met hadn't done much to alter his cynicism. Hell, maybe he hadn't given any a fair chance. Rubbing his forehead now, Nick knew he shouldn't be giving in to the lure of bitterness. He would simply swallow it and go to bed alone tonight, as he had most of the nights of his life.

And so would David, Nick thought cynically. But for David it wasn't fair. He hadn't seen their mother's perfidy, always engrossed in books and trusting others and a little vague. And so he didn't share Nick's pessimism. He'd fallen in love with Eliza, married her and begun raising kids. The union had been stormy for years—but they loved each other, that was clear. Still, she'd abandoned him for what she'd thought would be a better life.

On that day Nick's certainty that women weren't to be trusted was cemented.

Tracy was the first he'd thought of as a person deserving admiration as well as sexual desire. And he detested the idea.

Behind him he heard her voice, speaking in that low-toned, gentle way she used with the younger children, then heard Kitty's quiet answer. The two of them came into the room, hand in hand, headed for the downstairs bathroom.

"Of course I'll help you go to the potty," Tracy was saying. "But you're such a big girl now you can mostly go by yourself, can't you?"

Kitty murmured a reply and Nick, still at the foot of the stairs, felt his eyes narrow. Hating the new emotions engendered by Tracy, he knew only a need to lash out at her.

"Let her go by herself," Nick told Tracy harshly. "She's done it alone lots of times."

"I'm sure she has," Tracy answered. "But she's asked me to help and—"

"You're too soft on these kids, Tracy. Especially the boys. They're all going to turn into wimps if you keep coddling them like you do."

He ignored the bewildered widening of her eyes as she said, "Nick, I hardly think keeping Kitty company while she's potty training will turn her into a wimp."

"No? Well, it might." Sourly, Nick's mouth twisted.

"Kitty," Tracy told the little girl, keeping a wary eye on Nick as if he might succumb to violence if she took her gaze off him, "I'll wait for you right here until you come out. I want to talk with your Uncle Nick for a minute, okay?"

"Okay," the girl said, edging by the stern-faced man to go into the bathroom and close the door.

Tracy folded her hands, tilting her chin to meet his gaze in her dignified way. "You frightened her."

Nick hesitated, his long, brown fingers drumming on the railing. Already he loathed himself for the harsh tone he'd used in front of the child. "Sorry." Half twisting away, he started to climb the stairs but jerked when Tracy's fingers curled around his forearm. His muscles contracted at her touch.

"Sorry?" she burst out. "That was wrong! That little girl—*all* the kids, including my own, hold you in hero-worshipping awe. Don't you know that?"

He shrugged, hoping she would take her hand away and hoping she wouldn't. "So?"

"You have no right to hurt Kitty. She's just a child. And she's done nothing to you. If you have something against me or vice versa, then let's keep our animosity separate from the kids. All right?" Her fingers bit into his arm until he faced her again.

It was a mistake not to just walk away; he knew it the minute he let his gaze wander over her accusing features and down to her full breasts that heaved with righteous indignation. A hint of cleavage peeped from her prim, buttondown blouse. He felt a returning heat inflame his body. It raced along his veins, urging him in the most primeval sense to chase and to conquer.

He fought it. Narrowed, distrusting eyes focused on her face, Nick swore inwardly. She could do this to him without any of the practised teasing employed by the kind of women he was used to. Battling the desire to crush her in his arms and kiss her into mindlessness, Nick's tension doubled.

He goaded her with the first thing that came to mind. "It doesn't matter how I act. She'll grow up the same as all women do. You're all ready to leave the ones who care for you at the first sign of something better."

At that moment Kitty appeared between them and Nick watched Tracy kneel to scoop the small girl into her arms. "You're wrong," she told him, voice low and shaking. She hugged Kitty to her breast, some powerful defense mechanism at work. "I don't know where you get your crazy ideas about me—or about women—and I don't care. But I know this—I'd never abandon those who love me. Especially my children. Do you hear me, Nick Roberts? Never!''

She swept the child up and hurried upstairs to leave him staring after her. Alone now, his anger drained away, leaving only hollowness. He was sickened at what he'd said to Tracy and with the way he'd frightened Kitty. David's daughter had always held a special corner in his heart—so tiny and big-eyed and loving. He never should have allowed his frustration toward Tracy to spill over onto the child.

But one thing in their exchange stood out in his mind. During her fierce defence of her children, Tracy had hugged Kitty close—a child who wasn't even one of her own. And he would be willing to bet his best cow pony that Tracy wasn't aware of it. She'd already taken the leap from caring for her children and David's children, to encompass all five as just *hers*.

This thought, more than anything before, unsettled him. For a moment he considered the idea of a woman capable of loyalty. A woman who loved wholeheartedly, with infinite faith in her man. He imagined a woman a man would count on. A woman to share joys and sorrows and who'd want to give as good as she got.

With a derisive snort, Nick started up the stairs and called himself all kinds of fool. Now, *there* was a fantasy. He doubted the female had been born who understood the meaning of the word *faith*.

Still, as Nick mounted the long staircase to his bedroom, he was calmer and even more introspective. He had some hard thinking to do—he would have to figure out how to behave civilly to Tracy, since it appeared she would be around for a while. He would have to somehow curb the wild images of passionate lovemaking that surfaced whenever he looked at her.

Dropping to the bed, he yanked tiredly at his boots. He'd come up with something. Tomorrow.

Up all night nursing a sick Kitty and worrying over what to do about Kyle's antagonism, Tracy clamped the soft foam pillow over her head to drown out the intrusive sounds of a yowling cat. But the pillow only muted the sound, and it carried on so Tracy was forced to surface through layers of much-needed sleep.

Kitty must have eaten too much pie or she'd picked up some sort of stomach flu, because she'd thrown up several times during the night, crying for Tracy. It wasn't until near dawn that the child finally settled into deep slumber.

Sitting up, Tracy frowned. She pushed the wild tangle of sun-lightened hair from her face. The yowling sounded familiar. Not a cat, but Toby, carrying on in the bathroom that adjoined her bedroom. *Good Lord,* Tracy wondered, was he sick, too?

She swung tired legs over the side of the bed and hurried into the hall. She didn't bother with a robe since her granny nightgown covered her from head to wrist to toe.

In the bathroom doorway Tracy came to a sudden halt, frozen by an almost unbelievable sight greeting her. Bright, Saturday morning sunlight spilled through the high window, illuminating Toby, who was immersed in a clawfoot bathtub overfilled with bubbles and getting a vigorous washing from Nick. The rugged, macho cowboy was kneeling, his blue workshirt splashed and half-soaked from Toby's struggles, looking very *unrugged* and *unmacho* as he tried to shampoo the two-year-old's hair.

"Don't just stand there, woman, give me a hand with this wild Indian of yours," Nick said to her.

Tracy came into the room slowly. She stepped out of splashing distance and allowed herself a small smile. Toby squealed when he saw her and gave up yelling to start motoring a plastic boat around.

"Good morning," Tracy said, a soft smile stealing over her face. Perching on an upholstered bench in front of a long vanity mirror, she idly swung her leg. "I had no idea you were so into cleanliness for the kids, Nick. I wish you'd have told me before. We could arrange for you to give each child a morning bath in consecutive intervals." She counted off her fingers. "Toby could be at six, Kitty at 6:20. Then Brad—"

Tracy," Nick warned. "I'm not making this a habit. It's just that this morning...uh..."

"Yes?" She raised one brow.

He shrugged, sheepish. "Well, my little partner here kind of had an um...accident in his bed last night—being a big boy and not wearing a diaper any more, you know. And I knew you had a time of it with Kitty being sick, so I thought I'd pitch in and clean Toby up."

Tracy blinked in wonder. "You heard me up with Kitty last night?"

"Yeah."

"And...you figured I needed the sleep this morning?"

"Right." He rubbed the boy's back with a washcloth.

"Oh." Tracy found it difficult to deal with this courteous side of Nick, especially after their heated exchange the night before. She allowed her smile to grow and tried not to beam at him. It seemed Old Stone Face was human after all.

When Nick started pouring water over Toby's head, the boy began squalling again.

"No, not like that. Let him hold the cloth himself." Tracy came forward, taking the washcloth and giving it to Toby to press over his eyes. She leaned over the tub, scooping water into a cup to demonstrate. Toby promptly quieted, then giggled and put a chubby handful of bubbles on her sleeve. Tracy gave him a mock frown, pretending to be upset, then dropped more bubbles on his round tummy. Before she could react, Nick scooped up a bit and dabbed it on the end of Tracy's nose. Toby squealed in delight when Tracy looked up, startled, the bubbles attached in a clownlike bulb at the tip of her nose. Nick grinned.

She wiped it away, suddenly shy. This playful side of Nick was new, also. She didn't have the least idea of how to handle him. Tracy realized all at once that they were crouched so close her thigh pressed his. He didn't look so forbidding in this situation. He looked approachable and... lighthearted. She glanced into his laughing eyes, then lowered her gaze in confusion.

It was while her eyes were still lowered that Nick leaned over Toby's head to brush a whisper of a kiss across her lips.

Utterly shocked, Tracy stared at Nick. Never in a million years would she have guessed he would kiss her. Not over a tub filled with soapy bubbles. Not over a splashing toddler. But he had.

Without thinking, she lifted two fingers to her lips. They felt warm and moist and soft. "Why... why'd you do that?"

"Because you're so pretty." He smoothed clear water over Toby's fair back. The boy was busy playing peek-a-boo with his toes in the bubbles. Tracy swallowed, wondering what Nick's touch would feel like on her own bare skin...on parts of her body no man had touched for such a long time.

She swallowed again, this time convulsively. But her overriding emotion was one of odd pleasure. He'd kissed her with guileless affection... and she'd liked it.

"Nick," she began in an effort at stemming her too-imaginative mind, "where'd you get that scar?"

His gaze fell to the twisted flesh marring his forearm. "A horse trampled me. Back, oh, five—six years ago. I got peeled from the meanest bronc any self-respecting stock contractor would give his eye-teeth for. He was 'double tough,' that horse—meaning he was harder to stay on than most—and that's one of the things judges look for when awarding points."

"Oh." She frowned. She didn't want to ask about the accident. Questions like—How badly were you hurt? Why didn't you quit then? Are you crazy? Instead, she asked, "What else do the judges look for?"

"In the rider? Poise, style, balance on the horse, smooth spurring rhythm. In the horse, the judges want lots of bucking and twisting maneuvers. All that in eight seconds, too. That's all we riders get, eight seconds to pit man against beast."

At some point during his explanation she detected a thread of pride running through his voice. "Why?" she whispered, afraid she already knew the answer. She was horrified at the mental images of a half a ton of angry horseflesh stomping a man. "Why do you do it?"

His expression held faint surprise. "For the challenge."

She waited for him to continue and when he didn't she prodded, "That's all?"

He shrugged. "Sure."

"I can't understand that. I can't understand why you—why *anyone* would willingly put their lives at stake that way. In the arena you're at terrible risk."

He gave another shrug, this time aloof. "It's my life."

"But what about the people who love you?" All at once she was furious. The selfishness! The idiocy! "What about Millie and David and the kids—they'd all suffer if you were hurt or killed! What gives you the right to risk that?"

Nick grimaced, then pulled a fluffy towel from the rack and lifted the boy from the tub. He began patting Toby dry. Instead of answering Tracy's question, he posed another, "What sort of accident was it that killed your husband?"

Tracy dropped her gaze, thrown off balance. She struggled to answer. "Stock-car racing. Strictly amateur."

"Ah."

"He didn't care that it was dangerous, either." Bitterness tinged her voice. "All he wanted was to go even faster. The whole thing started innocently enough. He loved watching the Indianapolis 500, the Grand Prix and Daytona races on TV. Then he started attending nearby events on weekends. It didn't take long for him to become obsessed with fast cars, and at last that obsession went from observation to participation."

"He put his safety and your happiness at risk every time he drove, is that right?" Nick asked gently.

She gave him a tight frown. "Perceptive of you, Nick." She gathered up her son and carried him into his small bedroom. She didn't turn to see if Nick had followed. She knew he would.

"Oh, he was fast, too. Real fast. But not very good. The managers, other drivers, even spectators said he was reckless. That's how it happened—the accident. He took a turn too fast and too high in the curve. His wheel snagged another car and he spun out. They said there was a fire. The paramedics rushed him to the hospital, but it was too late." She squeezed her eyes shut, hugging Toby so tightly he protested and she set him on the bed. Grateful for something to do, she began dressing him.

For a time she kept her hands busy, not looking at Nick. When she chanced a look up she found him lounging in the doorway, watching, considering her. He straightened, coming over to tuck in Toby's shirt. "Tracy, nobody said professional sports like rodeoing and auto racing aren't dangerous. It's part of what makes them exciting and interesting. But no one wants to get hurt." He rubbed a shoulder, smiling wryly. "Believe it or not, I avoid pain at all costs, myself."

"But look at you." Tracy handed Toby a crayon and a pad of paper. She gestured sharply at Nick, still massaging his shoulder. "You've got at least two injuries that I've seen—your scar and that arm you're always rubbing."

He abruptly stopped the massage.

She went on, her voice rising. "I'd be willing to bet you've got a whole lot more that I can't see. Probably broken a lot of bones over the years, huh, Nick? And what else—a few more scars? Got any pins in your knees or hips?"

When he flushed Tracy knew she'd hit the truth. "I thought so. Why, you're practically broken down. How old are you, anyway? Thirty-three, thirty-four?"

"Twenty-eight," he corrected stiffly.

The remainder of her tirade withered in her throat. She couldn't believe he was so young—she was actually two years older! The way he rose stiffly from the breakfast table in the mornings, rubbed at his shoulder, the weathered, sun-squint lines fanning from the corners of his eyes all told of his vigorous life.

Tracy let her gaze fall. It was even worse than she'd thought. The wariness she'd felt around him increased twofold. Or maybe her original caution was simply returning after she'd foolishly lowered her guard. He was a man who craved excitement as much as she wished to avoid it. His kind couldn't be satisfied with anything as mundane as a wife and family. What was that old saying? Something like an old cowboy never settles down, he just rides off into the sunset.

Nick sighed. "I've got my shortcomings, I admit it. I know I can't travel the circuit forever. But at least I can admit my problems."

She eyed him suspiciously. "What is that supposed to mean?"

"When are you going to stop overprotecting your boys—and yourself?"

She gaped at him. "However did you get that idea?"

"It's obvious. And I say you're running scared. Because your husband was killed in an accident, you're afraid of taking risks—for either yourself or your children. You've gotten used to mollycoddling your kids." He grimaced. "You were even afraid of letting them near a saddle horse."

"I don't believe this." Tracy bustled out of Toby's room, her concealing nightgown flapping against her legs, and entered her room next door. She jerked open a drawer and yanked out the first top and jeans her hands touched. "I'm doing what's best for my boys and for me and you've managed to twist it all around."

She faced the doorway where he was standing and pointed an indignant finger at her chest. "*I'm* not the one putting my life in danger every day. *I'm* not the one flitting around the country year in and out to climb onto a bunch of vicious horses bent on my destruction. *I'm* not stiff when I wake up in the morning because my body's been battered to a pulp. There's no scars on me or pins in my joints because of some silly sport.''

Nick's frown grew thunderous as she'd gone on, and now he took two steps toward her. "No? Well, you may not be stiff physically, but you sure seem pretty uptight otherwise. Maybe some good old-fashioned fun would lighten you up. Maybe you could use a little excitement."

"I've had all the excitement in my life I can stand. Craig saw to that! What I want now is peace."

"Yeah? Well, if your life were a sight more peaceful it would be downright boring. If you'd—"

David appeared at the doorway, his concerned glance going from Nick to Tracy.

A mortified blush started at her neck and rose to spread over her cheeks. With David's appearance she was brought back to earth and her station here at the ranch with a jarring thud. It was wrong to assume too much given her position in the household. She was hired help, not family. "I'm going to take my shower now. If you'll excuse me."

Embarrassed and gathering as much dignity as she could, she brushed by Nick, who glared at her, and David, who stepped back with a confused smile.

The next morning Nick had again disappeared.

By the end of the day Tracy's curiosity had eaten away at her until she couldn't stand it a moment longer. She came right out and asked Millie where Nick had gone.

"Taking care of business, I guess," the older woman replied vaguely, and Tracy might have dismissed it from her mind if Millie's answer hadn't been accompanied by a mysterious smile. Tracy was sure Millie wasn't telling the whole truth.

When she'd scanned the morning newspaper, her eye had fallen on local cattle-rustling problems, and she wondered if Nick could be dishonest. When she reflected on the gentle kiss given by a good-natured, wickedly sexy Nick, she wondered if he might be visiting a girlfriend. When on the kitchen radio the local commentators discussed shady dealings in local politics, she wondered if Nick could be involved in that. As far as she knew, he could be doing anything!

David never said a word about where Nick had gone, nor did he even seem to notice his brother was missing. In the house he spent his time either romping with the kids or cloistered in his office. Though David was impeccably courteous and had shown her around the ranch, he carried a faint aura of sadness that tugged at Tracy's heart. She imagined that being abandoned by the woman he loved was traumatic.

When Nick returned the following evening and nobody said a word about it, Tracy's frustration grew. What was Nick *up* to?

At dinner she sensed that David was feeling particularly low. Trying to divert herself from wondering about Nick, she gave special attention to drawing David out. Between warnings to the kids not to play with their food, she asked about his and Nick's upbringing and he told her amusing stories about the devilry they'd gotten into as boys.

Relaxing as she'd hoped he would, David leaned back in his chair at the dinner table and related a tale. At the other end of the table Nick listened, saying little, a gleam of humor in his eyes. Tracy tried to avoid his gaze, giving full attention to David as he talked.

"Well, this calf got dysentery—that was the year that I was about fifteen, Nick about eleven—and after doctoring the little thing we set it free to rejoin it's mother, only he was rejected. She didn't recognize him anymore and didn't want anything to do with him. Then she got sick and died, poor thing."

Kyle stabbed at his baked chicken, spearing a forkful. "Did the calf die, too?"

"Nope. It probably should have, though. I guess we could have given him a mixture of condensed milk and water, but we didn't have to." David gestured at his brother with a thumb. "You see, that old son down there knew of another cow whose baby had died and who *would* want him."

Tracy's reluctant gaze swung to Nick. "But if his own mother didn't want him, how did Nick figure another cow would?"

Nick smiled, letting David answer. "That's what our daddy and his foreman kept telling him. But young Nick insisted that a cow whose calf died had been bawling and carrying on so hard he just knew she'd take to the orphaned baby." David paused dramatically, warmed to the telling. He flashed a mischievous grin at his brother. "You never knew my daddy, Tracy, but I can tell you he ran this spread with an iron fist. He knew cattle ranching from the inside out. He wasn't about to let any eleven-year-old boy—even a son of his—tell him to go about his business. He told the foreman to put the calf down."

Eyes wide, Brady sucked in a breath. "You mean... shoot him?"

"Yes, sir, I do. But Nick wouldn't give up. He snuck into the barn, getting the calf together with the new mama."

"Did she take the calf?" Brady asked.

David shook his head. "Sure as our daddy said, she didn't want him, either."

Kyle had stopped eating, his forkful of chicken forgotten. "Did...did the foreman end up shooting the calf?"

"Nope. Nick was really stuck on the notion of those two animals getting together. He got an idea. Sneaking back into the house, he snitched a spray bottle of our mother's best perfume. It smelled like spring flowers—she'd sent all the way to Dallas for it." David's voice lowered conspiratorially and Tracy leaned forward in her chair.

"Well, go on about the perfume," she prompted.

"He hid that bottle in the back pocket of his trousers but it stuck out, so he just knew he'd be caught. So he edged his way around Daddy and *backed* into the corral."

Tracy laughed. "Then what?"

David settled back into the chair. "Since cows identify their calves by smell, Nick figured he'd spray the calf with the perfume and then give the cow a noseful." He paused, drawing the tale out.

"And?" Tracy urged.

"And our daddy was just tickled because it worked. The cow came to accept the calf by that smell. Of course our mother wasn't too pleased about the use of her good perfume. She wanted to give Nick a hiding, but Daddy wouldn't let her. He said Nick had the makings of a fine rancher." He chuckled, shaking his head at the memory.

Tracy laughed, delighted. The children resumed eating, happy with the ending of the story. At his end of the table, Nick grinned, albeit sheepishly. She knew he was a bit embarrassed, but proud. He had every right to be, Tracy thought, her consternation with him warming to forgiveness. As she met his gaze the warmth increased.

The man had his surface faults, she allowed, lots of them. But deep down he was good. Good with the children, good at running the nuts-and-bolts end of the ranch. Even good at riding nasty broncs. And he looked good, too.

No, she amended, growing light-headed under his steady scrutiny, he looked *great*.

Over the heads of the children, their eyes locked. She felt more vulnerable each second, pinned by the rapidly heating hunger he allowed her to read in his face. It was curiously seductive, that hunger. It gave her a delicious sensation of power.

Tracy broke the bond, flustered. Abruptly, she pivoted in her chair to wipe Kitty's face. She fumbled with the napkin, dropped it twice, then laughed nervously to bend over and pick it up, only to bump heads with Dan, who was trying to help.

"Sorry." She tousled his hair gently, then snuck a peek back at Nick. The contrary man was calmly eating, eyes on his plate as if nothing had happened.

Nothing *had* happened, Tracy berated herself. She'd read far more into a simple meeting of eyes than she ever should.

Yet on the veranda an hour later, Tracy had to repeat her inner warning. Nick kept sending her sensual messages, then veiling his eyes moments later until Tracy came to the frustrating conclusion that he wanted her; he just didn't *want* to want her.

Confused by her reaction to him, Tracy tried to divert herelf by concentrating on an ancient issue of *National Geographic* and Millie's idle chatter. David and Nick were quietly discussing business, David relaxing in one of the wicker chairs, Nick smoking, half sitting on the edge of the railing.

Though the younger children were in bed, Tracy heard sounds in the family room of dice being thrown on a game board. The three boys seemed to get along fairly well, which was a relief.

A cloud of smoke wafted overhead. Tracy had to grit her teeth and forcibly restrain herself from staring at Nick. He leaned back, one leg bent, the other on the ground supporting most of his weight. A lean hand rested on one muscular thigh, the other held a casually drooping cigarette. Flicking an ash with careless ease, Nick took a drag, squinted, then shot another steaming glance at Tracy, slowly exhaling.

Tracy caught a breath at the sheer intensity in his eyes; she was beginning to think she might go up in smoke herself.

For just a moment she gave in to temptation and allowed her rapt gaze to scan over him. His habitual jeans and Western shirt fit snugly but well, faithfully following the sturdy lines of his hard shoulders and hips. He'd nudged his ever-present hat away from his face. But it was the potent sensuality radiating from him like waves of Montana heat that held Tracy enthralled.

During his talk with David, he never took his eyes off her for long, dragging his gaze over her face and down to her full breasts and trim waist and thighs. She felt as if she were being stamped with a smouldering brand.

Weakening rapidly, Tracy wondered at the meaning of it all. They had nothing whatever in common; she feared and hated his profession, was older than he by a good two years and had three kids most single men would view as added baggage. Springing from these differences was an animosity that couldn't be snuffed out.

They also had a strong dose of old-fashioned lust for each other, she acknowledged wryly. And lust had nothing to do with age or children or life-styles. She snorted inwardly at the direction her thoughts had taken. Nick Roberts didn't want anything lasting with her! A quick tumble in the hay was about as far as his thoughts went.

The idea brought her chin up in renewed determination to ignore him. She wouldn't be one of his buckle bunnies! She steeled herself for another of his sexy looks. He didn't keep her waiting.

A lull in conversation brought his gaze back to collide with hers. He was making no pretense now of concealing his thoughts. Male hunger...blatant sexuality—it was all there in the deep, tobacco-brown eyes—and he didn't care who saw it, Tracy realized with a start. Millie had taken up a pair of knitting needles and a ball of yarn, and David was peering at a book over his reading glasses. At any second either of them could look up and see what Nick didn't bother to hide.

With an abrupt movement, Tracy threw herself out of her chair and hurled the magazine aside. She wiped damp palms along the seat of her pants, announcing brightly, "I need some air. Excuse me." She didn't wait for a response, knowing only the driving desire to flee.

Blindly, she hurried down the steps and escaped into the night.

Chapter Five

It took all of Nick's considerable willpower to keep himself seated at the railing and not go chasing off after Tracy. Where was the logic in it? She was in a vulnerable position here as the nanny. If he made advances, she might fear all manner of repercussions: jeopardizing her job by refusing—jeopardizing her job by accepting. A relationship between them would be too complicated. A gentleman would have backed off, a sensitive man would have taken her avoidance at face value. It had been a long time since he'd been called either.

She was wary, frightened of him. Maybe she had good reason. Maybe he *would* leave her alone.

Sixty seconds later, Nick was drumming impatient fingers on the railing, eyes straining unconsciously into the night in search of her. His willpower was definitely not slipping, he insisted. But where had she gone? He wouldn't go after her, dammit. He shouldn't.

"Think I could use some air myself," he announced less than a minute later, echoing Tracy's words. He got to his feet and stretched with feigned weariness. Nodding, David was already immersed in his thick manual of modern accounting procedures.

Millie's deft fingers manipulated her knitting needles. She smiled at him, wide eyed. "It gets real stuffy in these screened-in veranda's all right."

Nick frowned, knowing good and well she was needling him; the veranda was never stuffy. At his dark scowl, Millie's smile merely widened. Turning away, he repressed a sigh. He never had been able to intimidate Millie. Or fool her.

He found Tracy in the main barn, standing in front of Jackson's stall. The horse was nuzzling her shoulder. "I don't have any apples tonight, boy," she was murmuring.

In the doorway, Nick paused, silent. Fresh scents of hay and horse blended with Tracy's elusive perfume. The overhead fluorescent lighting—a concession to the nineties—was off tonight, the building lit only by a single electric lantern hung on the wall. Soft light touched neatly hung stall shovels, rusty rakes and a rope lariat.

Tracy shifted her weight, scratching the buckskin's neck. The movement brought her honey-golden hair, hanging free, to curl about her shoulders into shining prominence under the lanternlight. A sudden urge to thrust his hands into the heavy mane gripped Nick. He took a step into the room.

Tracy whirled in surprise. "What—What are you doing here?"

Advancing, Nick lifted one large shoulder. "Depends."

"On what?" she returned, facing him like a skittish filly.

"On you." Nick approached until he stood mere inches away, his height forcing her to bend her head back in order to meet his gaze. He lifted a burnished strand of hair from her neck. In great interest he watched while she swallowed with difficulty. When she didn't move away, he felt a deep satisfaction. His eyes fell to her lips—lush and softly pink.

"What is it you want?" Her hazel eyes were cautious tonight.

"I'll say it, Trace." He let go of her hair to drop both hands onto her shoulders. "But I think you already know what I want. Don't you?"

Vehemently, she shook her head, straining away from his grip. "No," she whispered.

"I want you."

"No," she repeated. Her voice carried a touch of panic. She reached behind her back and pressed flat against the stout wood of the stall, as if it might give way and she would be able to run from him again.

Nick chuckled. "Don't look so shocked. You've known."

"Forget it, Nick," she insisted, seemingly unable to drag her eyes away from his. "It won't work. I'm not available and I'm not interested."

"I don't believe you." He closed the gap between them, leaning both hands at waist height beside her, caging her in. "Tell you what. I'll make you a deal. You agree to give me one little kiss, and if you don't like it, I won't bother you again. Okay?"

While he spoke, he consolidated his advantage and moved closer still—but not close enough to bring their bodies together. Her breathing shallow, Tracy put her hands on his chest and pushed. She shook her head. "Absolutely not."

He didn't move, he was unable to. Lured by hints of her violet-scented fragrance, he watched her, using every seductive technique he knew to draw her in—to challenge her, to dare her. She was a proud woman—he would use that pride to get what he wanted. In a flash of insight, Nick knew he would use anything at all to be able to kiss her right now. He *needed* to kiss her. In a deceptively soft voice, he baited, "Afraid?"

That brought her chin up. "Of course not. I told you, I'm not interested."

He felt his lips pull back in a wolfish grin. "Then what's the danger? Sure you're not scared?"

He watched in amusement while she struggled with her pride and her curiosity. She was attracted to him, he knew that. But he had to convince her—it was important, somehow, that she consent to his embrace. Hell, he could lean over right now and take her lips. But that wasn't the way he wanted it with Tracy. He wanted her to invite him.

"I'm not scared."

"No? Well, actions speak louder than words."

The struggle waging across her face was finally won by pride, and Nick hid a sigh of relief. He wasn't sure what he would have done if she'd refused. "One kiss," she informed him primly. "And when I tell you I don't like it, you'll leave me alone from now on, is that our deal?"

"I give you my word."

In charming confusion, she dropped her gaze from his. "Uh...all right." He thrilled when she sank tentative fingers into the worn cotton of his shirt, seeking his shoulders beneath.

Tracy gasped as Nick's mouth came down on hers. His hands went to the sensitive area of her lower back to urge her closer. She felt as if she were caught in a violent dust storm, her senses spinning so wildly that she had to cling to the only constant left in her world—Nick.

Not until that moment did she realize how badly she'd wanted the rough cowboy to take her in his arms. Now that it was happening, filaments of excitment began unfurling in her chest. They radiated to her toes and fingertips, vibrated through her like low-voltage electricity.

She heard him groan. He dragged her hips into the nest of his thighs, his big palms soothing in long, sweeping strokes from her shoulder blades almost to her rump. Tracy tried to arch away from the encroaching hands, only to find she was thrusting herself toward him instead.

Nick's barely controlled desire wove tendrils of temptation around Tracy. By degrees, she gradually surrendered to pleasure. Warm, his mouth was teasing, his tongue seeking hers suggestively, his sturdy chest and hips and jean-roughened legs branding heat and need along her body. His earthy scent made her think of tall ponderosa pines and warm chinooks and clear fishing streams. She inhaled as if the scent were oxygen itself.

It didn't take much imagination to fancy herself bound by emotional bonds as strong as those of the lariat on the wall.

Again and again he kissed her, his mouth leaving hers for only instants to drag over a delicate brow or leave a dampened path along her jaw. His beard-roughened cheeks scraped her skin, leaving a tingly awareness of their fundamental differences—his vibrant maleness to her soft femininity. She allowed him to take more of her weight, assuring herself fleetingly that in a moment she would wrench free. Not yet though, not yet....

Breathing faster, she was acutely aware of his hand as it slid between their bodies to rest on her ribs. His thumb was a fraction of an inch below the weight of her breast. Knees trembling, Tracy admitted to herself that if Nick were to step back now, she would collapse on the straw-covered floor in a heap.

To prevent that possibility, she moved one hand from his shoulder to wind around his neck. She thrust her fingers into the inviting thickness of his hair. Seeking his thundering pulse she brought her other hand to the tanned column of his throat. Its staccato beat matched her own. She shouldn't be doing this! a weak voice warned. He was danger and risk and foolhardiness.

But at his stifled gasp, she knew she'd pleased him with her response and felt a wonderful sense of pride. For Tracy, the world narrowed down to this moment, this man. She ignored the warning voice, pressed tiny kisses over his throat, murmured incoherent sounds of encouragement. He kissed her again.

It wasn't until Nick tore his mouth from hers and pushed her head into his shoulder that she began to surface through layers of sensual haze.

"Honey," Nick whispered hoarsely, "unless you want me to lay you down in front of this stall, we'd better stop right here." With an unsteady hand, he shoved his fingers into his hair and allowed his hold on her to slacken.

With excruciating slowness, Tracy began to realize the extent of her response. Eyes wide now, she kept still against his shoulder and stared at the lariat hanging innocently against the opposite wall. *What was she doing?*

Holding her away, Nick tried to capture her gaze, but she kept her head averted. She had no wish to see the triumph on his face. "Trace?" he whispered, and if she didn't know better, she might have imagined uncertainty in his voice.

"Go ahead," she bit out, studying the tips of her shoes, "go ahead and gloat. I guess you'll take a lot of pleasure out of making me eat my words."

Instead of answering, he surprised her by jerking her back into his arms and groaning. "Oh, God. I'm not going to gloat, honey. That was...wonderful. More than I'd ever dreamed. There's a lot of fire in you."

She eased back, chancing a look to see if he was teasing. He wasn't. "Thanks," she mumbled.

Since the tops of her worn tennis shoes could provide only so much interest, she slid her gaze to an aged wooden barrel in the corner, then restlessly on to a jumble of tractor parts one of the ranch hands was repairing. She knew her avoidance of Nick was obvious, yet she couldn't look at him. Her surrender to his kiss had been complete and abandoned. In light of her protests, it was embarrassing.

He tucked her hair behind an ear. "If there were any woman in the world I'd want to be getting involved with, it'd be you. You know that, don't you?"

"Involved?" She lifted her head, at last meeting his eyes.

He nodded, a tender expression softening his harsh features. "But I decided a long time ago I'm not the committing kind. I can't—I won't promise you anything."

"Promise me?" she echoed, feeling as if she could only repeat his words. What was he talking about? And who did he think he was? "What makes you think I—"

"Now, Tracy, don't get all upset on me, honey. It's just the way I'm made. I won't allow any woman to get the best of me. I've seen too many men made a fool of."

Tracy glared up at Nick, knowing her eyes were beginning to glitter with suppressed fury. "Why, you arrogant, egotistical—" She clamped down on the tirade rising in her throat and tried to swallow it. "I guess you're talking about David and Eliza, huh? Because of the way she left him, you believe all women are untrustworthy?"

He nodded readily. "That situation does stick out in my mind, among others."

"By others I suppose you mean your mother?" Tracy guessed.

Immediately, Nick's eyes went cold. He stiffened. "You don't know anything about my mother."

Tracy backed away, keeping a careful eye on the leashed violence she saw in his face. "It's true I'm not well versed in your family history. But I know enough to see her actions have left their share of scars."

At his sides Nick's hands curled into fists. His eyes narrowed. "Shut up, Tracy."

"Okay. I won't discuss anyone but us. Yes," she went on recklessly, unable to bank her anger. "Let's talk about *us*. It appears we have a misunderstanding here, Nick. Tell me if I'm off the mark, but because you've kissed me one time, you think I expect some sort of...commitment from you? You're assuming I want a *relationship* with you?" She waited, a hand on her hip.

He gave a tight shrug. "Don't you?"

"Oh, for pity's sake!" All at once she wanted to scream in frustration. She hated his arrogance. She never wanted him to know how intense her reaction had been. She knew if he discovered the extent of her need for him he would destroy her. "Because of one kiss?"

A corner of his mouth kicked up. "It was a pretty terrific kiss."

She tried for her coldest smile. "So?"

"I can separate the physical side of life from the rest as easily as anyone else—if that's what you mean. I'm certainly not in love with you. But, honey," he drawled, letting his eyes slide down her body, "I sure do want you."

"That's too bad," she said, mingled anger and hurt forming an agonized knot in her chest. "Because you won't have me. Now or ever." She whirled and started for the door.

He reached out to grab her upper arm. "Let me tell you something else."

"What?" she answered tightly, knowing that in his present mood he would never let her go until she heard him out.

"David won't marry you, either."

Tracy gasped. "I would never have expected him to," she said indignantly.

"Is that so?" He studied her with a cocked head, and she knew he didn't believe her.

"I came here to take care of the children. To make a new life for myself and mine. Not to get married. I'm not even attracted to David," she added.

"No? Maybe to a woman in your position that wouldn't matter much."

"Oh! Of all the low-down, insulting comments you've made to me, that was the worst! I'm not a—a gold digger! If I were, why would I be kissing you?"

He grinned contemptuously. "As I said before, needs can be separated. Financial ambition and physical gratification are two different things."

Tracy felt the blood drain from her face. In a low, hoarse voice that made her throat ache, she whispered,

"Do you realize you're likening me to a woman of the street?"

"If the shoe fits...."

More furious than she'd ever been in her life, Tracy clamped down on the denial begging to be unleashed and strode jerkily for the door. She threw it back so hard the heavy wood crashed into the wall and rattled on its hinges. Outside, the night was cruelly dark. Bleak shadows from an insipid moon cast eerie shapes over the barn.

Halfway to the house she dashed at the tears streaking over her hot cheeks. She didn't even notice Nick beside her until he grabbed her shoulders and brought her to a forced halt.

"Trace, wait. Look, I'm...I'm sorry, all right? I didn't mean any of that."

"Let me go," she ground out between gritted teeth.

"Not until you listen." He released one of her shoulders to stab impatient fingers through his hair. "I shouldn't have said what I did. It was wrong."

She strained against his hold. "Get out of my way, Nick!"

"No, listen to me. What I said was insulting, and it wasn't true. Honestly, I don't know what got into me."

It was his expression of genuine confusion that finally got through to her. She drew in a breath so deep it hurt. "Why *did* you say it, Nick? What have I done to give you such a low opinion of me?"

"Nothing, I swear! I guess I was trying to hurt you."

"Whatever for?" Through tear-blurred eyes, Tracy searched the deep shadows playing over his face.

He sighed hard. "I'm not sure exactly. Maybe because you hated responding to my kiss so much. To a man, that's not too flattering."

Tracy stared at him, relaxing slightly. She hadn't realized he could be vulnerable. In the long run, though, it wouldn't matter. She said as much. "There's a reason for that. I don't want to be associated with a man who craves excitement and has so little regard for his own safety. It strikes too close to home."

"I do regard my safety," he defended, sidetracked. "I've lived this long, haven't I?"

"What about all your injuries?"

"They're nothing I can't handle."

"Just mere trifles? Incidents?" she offered sarcastically.

His gaze was hard. "Right."

Tracy thew up her hands. "See? Anything between you and me won't work. At least we're in agreement about that." She tried to quiet the wail in her voice.

"That's a cop-out," he said.

Exasperated, Tracy let her gaze run over his lean frame as she marshalled her arguments. Craig had been tall and lean, too, she remembered bitterly. He'd also been a risk taker. "Let me ask you something," she said, folding her arms. "What specifically about the rodeo draws you?"

Blinking at the unexpected question, Nick thought for several seconds. "The skill. The excitement. Adventure. The uncertainty. The—"

"Ha!"

"Ha, what?"

"You just said the uncertainty."

"So? I said other things, as well."

"But uncertainty is the only thing that doesn't fit! Don't you see? Crowd pleasing and danger are in your blood—you love performing—pitting yourself against the odds. I'll bet you were a lion-wrestling gladiator in another life!" Nervous tension made her words fast and breathless. "In order to please a crowd, one must put himself at risk! All those people come to see you get hurt. They don't want you to succeed—they want blood!" Shaking violently, Tracy realized dimly that she was losing what little control she had. She covered her eyes with her hands.

"No," Nick was saying, forcing her hands away from her face. "Some do, I'll admit, but most spectators want to see skilled horsemen perform. Saddle-bronc riding is only one part of the rodeo. There's barrel racing and roping and—hey, you ought to be glad I don't go in for steer wrestling or bullriding."

Tracy looked at him with horrified eyes.

"Listen, I'm good at what I do, I like it. I know the life. And I'm luckier than most. I get to come back here—" he swept his arm in a wide arc "—when I need a break. What I can't understand is your attitude. You can't play it safe all your life, Trace. Seems to me since the death of your husband you've been running from everything."

"You've said that before."

He gave a curt nod. "And now you're trying to run from us."

Tracy half turned, offering only her profile. Suddenly she was exhausted...so tired of arguing. "I don't understand you. Just a moment ago *you* were telling *me* you didn't want to get involved. Look, I just want some peace, that's all. I want to be free of anxiety." She swung back to face him, knowing the vulnerable expression in her eyes might betray her, knowing her voice was pleading. "Please understand, Nick. If I start caring for you, I'd never know true happiness. I'd worry about you. I don't want to have those kinds of worries ever again."

A pained grimace drew Nick's face tight. "I don't believe this."

"So," she finished bravely, "You see, you and I have nothing left to say to each other." With that she went into the house and up the stairs.

Chapter Six

Inside, Tracy bade quick good-nights to David and Millie, helped pack away the board game and ushered the boys upstairs to bed. Kyle avoided her eyes and she sighed, too tired to wonder what she should do about his antagonism.

In her own room, she donned her granny gown and lay beneath the covers staring at the open-beamed ceiling. Instead of simmering with anger for the cruel words Nick had flung at her, she couldn't stop replaying the passionate kiss they'd shared. Why wasn't she furious with him? His simple apology couldn't take back the hurt he'd caused.

Images flashed before her mind's eye: the shadowy barn, Nick's unfamiliar, excitingly strong frame pressed into hers, his intense, hungry eyes, his obvious desire for her. Graphic details mingled with the hazy sensuality she'd experienced when he'd held her—as if she'd been swimming and had, for a few moments, gone beneath the water's surface.

On a muffled groan, Tracy remembered the wanton way she'd leaned into Nick. The fact that he'd been equally eager did her pride no good at all. The very idea that she'd succumbed to the adolescent dare he'd thrown out was unbelievable!

Yet, if she hadn't been tempted, she never would have succumbed in the first place, argued her tiny voice of reason. She'd wanted his embrace, Tracy admitted—and his kiss.

Rolling onto her side, she drew her knees up under the hand-stiched quilt and allowed herself the luxury of remembering.

It was a long time before she fell asleep.

Two heavy saddlebags were sitting on the dining room table directly in front of her usual seat when Tracy appeared with Kitty and Toby the next morning.

She peeked inside to find packages of Millie's special milehigh roast beef sandwiches and shiny red apples. It looked like someone was planning an outing on horseback. For just a moment Tracy allowed herself to imagine just she and Nick, galloping across the prairie. She could almost feel the hot sun and the even hotter tobacco-brown of his eyes on her skin.

Shaking herself, she sighed. The long night of sensual fantasies comprised wholly of undulating kisses in Nick's arms had done nothing to strengthen her resolve against him. She pushed two English muffins into the toaster and got out canteloupe for slicing.

Just then, Millie bustled into the kitchen, snapped an apron from a rack and tied it behind her back. "Beautiful morning, isn't it?" she sang out, pouring milk for the children. "How I love Sundays. Just right for a picnic, too." Before Tracy could say a word, she went on, "And don't you worry about a thing. Kitty and Toby and I are going to have us a grand time! We're going to bake cookies and watch *E.T.* on videotape. I always cry in the middle of that movie. Anyway, I've already told Nick it's all right, so don't you argue."

"Argue?" Tracy answered weakly, dropping into a chair.

"And," Millie rushed on, "David is taking the big boys on a tractor ride today, so you see you have nothing to worry about. You've been here weeks already and never taken a day off. It's a shame—a young woman like you all cooped up here with no company your own age. When he mentioned it, I told Nick a picnic was a terrific idea!" She beamed at Tracy, who was smiling wryly.

"Terrific," Tracy repeated. Any thought of arguing faded like prairie dust devils in the face of Millie's enthusiasm.

Millie was right, Tracy decided, giving in and feeling more lighthearted than she had in days. She *did* need a day off, and a nice trail ride with a homemade lunch at the end might be lovely. Vivid images of the seductive man who would be sharing the day had to be snuffed out. It was just a ride, she assured herself, gazing eagerly out the window at the beckoning sunlight and azure skies. Nothing more. Just a ride.

Alone with a magnificent man she was too weak to resist.

Less than two hours later Tracy wound up back in Nick's arms. The long ride to their destination—a meandering creek flanked by spreading shade willows and picnic grounds—had been uneventful, pleasant and friendly.

If one could call a deliberate brushing of his hard knuckles over her soft cheek uneventful. If one thought of blazing eyes that shot clear sensual messages, just pleasant. If one supposed an easy lifting of feminine weight by masculine hands into a saddle, merely friendly. Nick, it seemed, was bent on seduction.

Tracy shivered in spite of the day's heat. She tried diverting herself by drinking in the surrounding land. On the range they passed shallow gullies, high buttes and wide flats. Prairie vegetation of bluebunch wheatgrass and spiky rough fescue sprang from crevices between boulders. She breathed in the spicy smell of sagebrush, then traded the leather reins from her right hand to her left.

Nick had chosen for her the braided bridle she'd admired in the tack room—she'd recognized the workmanship right away and thanked him, oddly touched by his thoughtfulness. He'd given a satisfied nod as if indicating he was glad she noticed.

Though her docile roan mare had a gentle, rolling gait, Tracy felt the small muscles in her pelvis and lower back begin to ache from the unaccustomed exercise. She shifted a little in the saddle.

Sighing to herself, Tracy admired Nick's proud carriage as he sat the big gray gelding. Nick looked fantastic atop a horse—all long, lean, Stetson-hatted cowboy. She sighed again, dragging her eyes away and asked him about the upcoming fall roundup.

He slowed until the horses walked side by side. "It's a sight," he replied with a grin. "And a lot of work."

Tracy patted the mare's shiny neck. "I've never seen a branding. I suppose rounding up all those cattle and then throwing and tying them takes a long time."

"We don't throw them anymore. Most of the bigger ranches use squeeze chutes now."

At Tracy's questioning look, Nick elaborated. "A squeeze chute is a V-shaped metal trough in which the calf is clamped against one side. The side tilts to form a branding table. Then he's branded and innoculated against disease." Nick chuckled. "Like any modern contraption, it doesn't always work. Some escape and we *do* have to catch 'em and throw 'em down."

"It sounds exciting."

Nick patted his shirt pocket and then dropped his hand, as if searching for cigarettes but changing his mind. "I don't know about 'exciting,' exactly. But it's a busy time for us. And it's loud."

"Loud?"

"Sure. Through the branding process, the cows have to be separated from their calves, and they don't like it a bit. They all set up such a bellowing and a bawling you wouldn't believe it."

"I can imagine how a mama cow would feel—forcibly separated from her baby and sensing he's going to get hurt somehow."

A teasing light glinted in his eye. "Kind of like all that bellowing you did at me when Brady fell off the buckskin?"

Tracy colored lightly. She was amazed to find she really enjoyed Nick's company. He was interesting and thoroughly charming when he wanted to be. He had a good sense of humor, too, in spite of the fact that he seemed to direct it mostly at her.

"You bring the kids out to watch the branding," Nick offered. "We'll be starting at the end of next week."

"Kyle and Brady and Dan begin school Monday."

"They won't miss anything," Nick reassured her. "We go from sunup to sundown for days on end." He shifted position, his saddle creaking, and he flashed her a small smile. "Right about then I'll probably be too tired to kiss you much."

Tracy flushed dark pink at his words. She dug her heels into the startled mare's flanks and took off at a quick canter. Nick kept pace beside her, his rangy gelding striding out easily. Tracy refused to meet Nick's eyes.

Up ahead a stand of alders appeared, interspersed by swaying willows. Before she knew it they'd entered the ranch's private picnic grounds and she held her horse to a walk then stopped to admire the clear water of the creekbed and the shady trees nearby.

Nick dismounted, raising his big hands to circle her waist and ease her down. Her palms at his shoulders, she slid slowly, slowly along the length of his body until her toes barely touched ground. Her thighs, her hips, her breasts aligned and burned against his solid frame.

"Thank you," she offered in a strangled whisper.

He grinned wickedly at her for a long moment. At last he stepped back, touching the brim of his hat. "Mighty welcome."

After he untied the saddlebags of food and hobbled the horses, he spread a red flannel blanket beneath a drooping willow and began setting out the food. Tracy joined him, letting out a sigh of relief as she settled on the ground with her knees tucked under. It had been years since she'd been on a horse and her muscles were trembling with fatigue.

"Take a couple aspirin and a hot bath tonight and you'll be good as new," Nick said, handing her a sandwich and a can of soda.

"Is it that obvious?" Tracy asked, accepting the food. "I'll take your advice, but I'm afraid it'll be a few days before I'm over this soreness. We still have to ride home, too." She took a bite. "It's funny, but as a kid I don't remember getting this sore."

"Naw, kids don't. Their muscles are pretty pliable."

"I guess so. The boys haven't complained once about any muscle aches, even though they've ridden almost every day since we got here." She hesitated, lowering her sandwich. "Nick, I've been wanting to thank you for my sons' riding lessons. They...they think a lot of you. I've already told you, you're their hero."

"Your sons," Nick said, dismissing most of what she'd said and rolling the words around on his tongue. "How does it feel, Trace, to be a parent? To have sons." He leaned back against the trunk of the willow, chewing his sandwich and studying her.

Glancing at him, Tracy wondered at his question. Could he be feeling the lack of a family of his own? A wife and children belonging just to him? Or was he simply curious—an emotionless outsider looking into the window of someone else's life?

She drew a breath, wondering if she would ever understand him. "I won't say it's been easy. Children are a lot of hard work and strained patience and sacrifice. But then there's also a baby's first steps, his scrapes and his smile after getting reassured. And mostly there's an unshakable love between parent and child." She smiled. "Of course I'm biased, but I think my three are terrific."

"They are, Trace." Nick leaned toward her, his expression intense. "They're the best. You've done a good job raising them."

"They're not raised yet." She kept her tone light.

"No, they're not," he agreed. "They need a daddy."

She glanced at him sharply, but he was polishing an apple on a cloth napkin. Carefully, she said, "I guess all kids deserve two parents. But sometimes it doesn't work out that way."

Restless, Tracy got up and moved a few feet away to the edge of the creek. Through the leaves of the willow, sunshine played on the water's surface in a shifting, dappled pattern. She stared at the water, thinking about Craig and where they would be in life now if he'd lived.

She was deep in thought when Nick came up behind and drew her back against his chest. He ran his fingers soothingly down her arms and back up to run them through her hair. Chin atop her head, he linked his hands about her waist.

It felt wonderful, she thought. Nice.

Slowly, a languor born of warm sun and strong embracing arms stole over Tracy. Her eyelids drooped as she sighed.

Exactly when he started nibbling along the sensitive line of her neck, she wasn't sure. Without thinking, she lifted her chin, offering him better access. She didn't want to consider all the reasons why she shouldn't allow herself to enjoy Nick's embrace. She was tired of waffling. The push-pull of frustrated sensuality had finally worn her down until she was willing to throw caution to the winds. At least temporarily.

Her last thought before Nick turned her in his arms for his kiss was that he must certainly sense her surrender.

One part of Tracy felt the soft breeze weaving through the graceful branches of the willow; she was aware of the nearby creek and its quiet gurgle. Though the sun beat only gently on her skin, she felt as if her senses were riding on overload in Nick's arms.

He both filled her with pleasure and made her acutely aware of a great hollowness within. His mouth slanted tenderly over hers, offering a kind of easy banked passion. He coaxed and teased and wooed. Tracy was enthralled.

Never had a man taken the time or trouble to try and win her with tenderness. Never had a man given before he'd taken.

When Nick broke the kiss, Tracy gave a little cry. But he bent to sweep her high against his chest and carry her to the blanket. Once there, he laid her down, pillowing her head on his scarred forearm, splaying his other hand possessively over her abdomen.

"Trace," he began, voice uneven, "If you don't want this to go further, stop me now."

"Can't we..." She hesitated, breathless, then finished in a small gush. "Can't we make just a little love?"

She was relieved when he chuckled. "Depends on what you mean. For instance, some might take that as an invitation to touch you here." He cupped the underside of her breast while his eyes held hers steadily. "Others might suppose you mean this would be okay." He began unbuttoning her blouse. "Still another may think you'd like this." He spread open her blouse and leaned to press his mouth over the white satin bra covering her nipple.

Lost, Tracy curled into him. She tried, without success, to stifle a moan. She had no words to tell him, so caught up in pleasure. Instead, she showed him, arching slightly and holding his head to her breast.

God help me, she thought, gasping at the radiating sensuality Nick engendered with his touch. The slight tremor in his hand as he caressed her only served to heighten her excitement. Only a man who cared deeply for a woman would be moved enough to tremble, she told herself on a soaring note of hope.

Like the endless whisper of the nearby water smoothing over rocks, Tracy felt passion for Nick flow and build. His moist breath heated her breast, dampening her bra, puckering her nipples in the slight breeze. Dragging back to her lips, he left a trail of hungry kisses along her neck and jaw. Again, he claimed her lips, and his hand covered her blossoming breasts.

She sighed his name, "Nick...."

He answered hoarsely, his words surprising her. "Dammit, Tracy, I know." With an unsteady hand he rubbed at his forehead and closed his eyes.

"Wha—"

"Don't say it," he insisted. "This isn't right, me taking liberties like this. I'll stop. I know you want me to."

Up on her elbows, Tracy tried to assimilate the meaning of his words. She felt disoriented, vague. "Stop?"

"Just let me get my breath. God, woman, you'd tempt a saint." He rolled onto his back and threw a shading forearm over his eyes. "If only you knew how difficult it is to call a halt right in the middle of lovemaking. It's just that you're so damned hard to resist." Below his concealing arm Tracy saw his sheepish grin. "Guess the cold showers I've been taking lately aren't going to do much good anymore."

Bemused, Tracy stared. So he *was* affected. Maybe as much as she, and not just physically. He most likely didn't realize it yet, but he felt more for her than simple lust. The underlying affection in his words told her that.

The trouble would be convincing him to recognize it. Given his deep distrust of women in general, she held out very little hope that he ever would. Maybe she shouldn't yearn for it.

The thought sobered her. She sat up, adjusted her clothing and curled her arms about her knees. "Why are we here today—you know, together? You didn't even invite me. Not really. You simply arranged for the children to be taken care of so I'd be free."

"I didn't want you to say no." He picked at a bit of grass.

"But why, Nick?"

"I wanted your company."

"Last night you said you wouldn't get involved with anybody."

He frowned. "I know. Lately my thinking's changed so much and so fast I can't keep up with it."

He fell silent. Tracy guessed it was as much of an explanation as she was going to get.

"Perhaps we'd best start back," she said, not looking at him. "I've got to take the kids off Millie's hands—she'll be getting tired about now." Deliberately, Tracy interjected mention of the children as a wedge of reality between them.

"Yeah," Nick replied, getting to his feet in one lithe movement. He didn't offer to help her up, and she was glad, knowing how explosive was their touching.

The packing up and mounting was done in awkward silence. She avoided his eyes, too confused and full of doubt to face him. On the long ride back she tried not to think about who had halted the lovemaking—of how Nick mistakenly assumed she'd wanted him to.

Face averted to hide her furious blush, Tracy knew she'd been willing to give Nick everything. In her haze of violent desire, it never occurred to her to stop. *He* had been the noble one. He had been the one to recognize a dangerous situation and pull back. He had had the foresight to think of the consequences. Not her.

The fact embarrassed her to no end. She drew a shaky breath and let the mare pick her own way over the pocked rangeland. Nick had certainly been every bit as affected as she—the evidence of his arousal had been blatant.

Tracy supposed she ought to thank him. Because what would have been the outcome of their consummation? Hiding a snort of disgust in a cough, she berated herself. Did she think that afterward Nick would instantly offer marriage? Did she suppose he would suddenly claim undying love?

Unexpected tears welled and threatened to spill. An acorn-sized knot of despair rose so hard and painful in her throat she was forced to swallow. By dint of will, she pushed her emotions back until they waited, at bay, to beseige her another time. She didn't want to marry Nick Roberts—why was she even thinking of it?

The thought made her angry and sad at the same time. She shot a resentful glance at Nick's stern profile. *He* was the root of all her problems. Her boys already loved ranch life. They were excited to be starting school in just a few days. Kitty and Toby, though they occasionally fought tug-of-wars over toys, had adopted each other as brother and sister. Tracy thought of the way Kitty often ran up to Toby in delight and yelled, "Toady!" And the shy way Toby was beginning to share his cookies with her. Tracy thought of Brady's and Dan's respect for Kyle's superior knowledge of riding and ranching. She thought of all her children's growing love for David and Nick and Millie.

And lastly, she thought of her own budding dream coming true of finally finding a *home*. Leaving Roberts Ranch would be a terrible blow to all of them. Tracy almost couldn't imagine it.

There was nothing to do, she decided on a fierce note of determination, but to forcibly ignore her attraction to Nick. She squared her shoulders. If she were cool to him, rebuffed him a time or two, he would get the message. Nick was smart. He'd soon find another to woo.

He need never know how deeply he'd tapped into her emotions. He didn't need to know how close she'd come to falling in love with him—a man whose reckless lifestyle she hated!

Tracy sat very still in the saddle. Love? No, it couldn't be. She was simply experiencing some very basic biological urges. Quite common, actually. Possibly to make herself feel better, she'd deluded herself into believing that Nick was capable of a long-term relationship. Of love.

She shook her head at the idea. Nick had informed her in no uncertain terms that he didn't want to get involved. She would be a fool to tell herself otherwise.

At the ranch, Tracy dismounted awkwardly because of her fatigued muscles, tossed the reins to a stableboy and hurried toward the house. She managed a mumbled thanks to Nick. He merely nodded, watching her go with a thoughtful, serious expression.

Inside the house, Tracy discovered they'd arrived back earlier than she'd thought and Toby and Kitty were still napping. The older boys had returned with David and were sprawled on the back steps of the kitchen, eating cool watermelon. She greeted them and Kyle refused to answer.

Safe in her room, Tracy avoided facing her worst fear—if this volatile attraction between her and Nick continued to build, she might have to leave the ranch.

Tracy moved to the small chest of drawers and attempted to calm herself by brushing her hair. She'd best put Nick out of her mind and concentrate on her job. Anyway, the problem of Kyle's antagonism needed attention, and soon. *You're not my mom!* pretty much summed up his feelings, she guessed.

From the beginning she'd noticed that Kyle had been quiet, even a bit standoffish. But she'd attributed it to natural reserve. She thought in time he would relax.

It seemed the other night when she'd served the blackberry pie, something had triggered a repressed resentment for his mother, and he was taking it out on her. Tracy grimaced. She had a real problem. Kids didn't respond well to rationalizations; they saw situations in black and white. Kyle's mom had abandoned Kitty and him, and now a new woman had arrived to take her place. In his mind, that wasn't right.

Simple.

The trouble would be in convincing him that Tracy wasn't taking Eliza's place—that she never could.

Complicated.

But she would have to try. She would talk with him—make him see that what he was feeling was normal and that she could help him.

Feeling better now that she had some sort of plan, Tracy went in to see if Toby had awakened yet. She would succeed at this job, she thought stubbornly, if it was the last thing she did. And she wouldn't let any plain, old-fashioned lust for Nicholas Roberts get in her way!

* * *

Observing Nick gentle a half-wild young sorrel to saddle a few days later in the large corral, Tracy at last began to understand his fascination in working with such an animal. She hadn't sought him out. She didn't want to see him. She and the kids had come only to play with the kittens.

Even had she wanted to seek him out, it would have been impossible. He'd pulled another of his disappearing acts and been gone without explanation for a day and a half.

Holding Kitty and Toby by the hand, Tracy peered through the rails, perversely unable to take her eyes off Nick. He coaxed the skittish colt to accept two filled burlap bags slung across his back. Balking at the unaccustomed weight, the colt nervously backed up, gave a little hop and yanked at the sheepskin-covered halter held in Nick's firm hand.

"Come on, Parjet, this won't hurt a bit. You just relax, little guy, and let me show you what to do." Nick's low voice soothed with quiet patience. His hands were steady and calm as he ran them and another burlap bag, this one empty, over the sorrel's body. After several moments the horse still danced nervously but tried only halfheartedly to pull away.

By the barn door several kittens were romping in the sunshine and Tracy encouraged Kitty and Toby to play with them. In this way she would be able to keep an eye on the children and watch Nick at the same time. At last Nick managed to convince the colt to follow his lead. Long after Tracy would have given up, Nick continued to talk to the horse, urging him with gentle, confident tones to become accustomed to the weight on his back and the bands over his nose.

He led Parjet to where Tracy stood on the opposite side of the fence. He tipped his hat. "Afternoon."

She nodded, wary and uncertain of him since the picnic. She shouldn't have let her curiosity about his training techniques intrigue her. He might think she was still interested in him. Staring off at some middle distance, she tried appearing nonchalant.

Nick stroked the horse's muzzle. "Ever see a horse broken to saddle before?"

"No. I—I'm a little surprised at your methods, though."

"Really?" One of Nick's heavy dark brows rose. "Did you think I'd take a whip to a horse, or maybe hog-tie him until he was cowed into doing what I wanted?"

Tracy gave him a fulminating glance. "Of course not. I just thought you'd use a more direct route. Something like strapping a saddle to his back, leaping on and letting him buck it out."

Nick adjusted the burlap bags and Parjet stamped, but was otherwise quiet. "That's one way to do it. And not a bad way, either. My method just takes a little longer. I think it makes for a better horse in the long run. It's called 'gentling.'" He looked Tracy full in the eyes, sending a subtle message she tried to ignore.

Feeling vaguely put in her place, Tracy stirred the toe of her worn tennis shoe in the dirt. Just then Parjet reached out with his head, snuffling along Nick's plaid workshirt. The movement had all the earmarks of an animal seeking affection from his master.

Tracy watched. "I can understand why you love ranch life and even working with a horse like Parjet. But for the life of me, I can't figure out your fascination in performing in the rodeo." She cocked her head, waiting for his answer with genuine interest. With some surprise, she realized she really *did* want to know.

Absently, Nick stroked the horse's long mane. He looped the reins around a post. "Have you ever given a lecture to a lot of people or maybe sung or danced or in some way performed for others?"

"A school play." Tracy smiled. "In third grade I played a daisy whose line was, 'All the children of the earth need love.' Except, I was so excited to be on stage with my parents and all the audience watching that I flubbed my one and only line, instead saying, 'All the love of the children need earth.'"

Nick chuckled.

"You laugh," Tracy said, rolling her eyes with remembered chagrin. "Everybody else did, too." She smiled at the memory. "It made me feel good, though, to make people laugh."

"It made you feel good," Nick repeated, pointing out her key remark. "The rodeo is show business, Tracy, and I'm a performer trying to entertain people while executing exciting feats of skill." He absently rubbed his shoulder, as she had seen him do many times. "There's an adrenaline rush, Trace, a thrill when the crowd roars— all because of what I'm doing in the arena."

In a quiet voice Tracy said, "Do you realize that while you're telling me this, you're rubbing your sore shoulder? The one you've obviously injured while performing these same exciting and sometimes dangerous feats of skill?"

Nick dropped his arm, a sheepish expression stealing over his hard features. "Sometimes it bothers me. Sometimes the aches and pains get to me and I wonder if it's time to stop...."

In mild astonishment, Tracy stared at him. "Have you really given any thought to quitting?"

"Sure. Over the years I've thought about it. Lately I've hardly been able to *stop* thinking about it." He draped an arm over the top rail, bringing them closer together. "There are other things I want to accomplish. Other priorities take precedence, eventually, in a man's life."

Tracy stifled a gasp when Nick reached through the rails to idly lift her hand. She felt his callouses rasp over her knuckles. He grinned, tugging her closer. She resisted, but not vigorously, safe in the knowledge that with the fence between them, Nick wouldn't be able to corral her completely.

What had he been implying about "other priorities"? Tracy wondered, growing frantic when Nick crushed her illusion of safety by reaching through with his other hand. He urged her closer until their faces were but a hairbreadth apart.

"Trace," Nick began softly, "now let me ask *you* something."

Riveted by his eyes and his hands and her own helpless fascination, Tracy gave a wary nod.

"You're a relatively young woman. You're of sound body and mind. Have you ever thought about having another child?"

Tracy swallowed. "Absolutely not. I'd never bring a baby into the world out of wedlock."

"What if you were married?"

"I'm not."

"But what if you were?" His fingers tightened on her elbows.

She tried to drop her gaze, tried to look away. She tried, and failed. Nick's compelling gaze ensnared her as surely as his arms held her immobile. "I—I—"

Before she could formulate an answer, Nick closed the distance between them and covered her lips with his own.

"No!" a voice screamed, and for a dazed second she thought it was her own until she realized it carried the shrillness of a little boy's frustrated anger.

Twisting out of Nick's arms, Tracy faced Kyle. He stood before them, face red with furious childish resentment. "You—*you stop it*," Kyle insisted, glaring at her.

"Kyle," Nick began warningly.

"I don't want you doing that stuff with my Uncle Nick," Kyle went on. "I don't like you fooling around behind my father's back!"

Aghast, Tracy put a hand on Kyle's shoulder, which he promptly shook off. "Kyle, you don't understand. I'm not fooling around on your father, honey. He and I aren't—"

With immature determination, Kyle pressed both ears with his hands, shutting out her explanation. Giving a sob, he pivoted and ran toward the house.

Instinctively Tracy started after him. She was brought up short as Nick yanked on her arm. "Leave the boy alone," Nick told her. "Let him cool off."

"But he thinks David and I—"

"I know what he thinks. I heard him."

"I've got to find him! I've got to explain that his father didn't bring me here for him and I to—to... Kyle has obviously jumped to a wrong conclusion and now resents seeing me with, er with... you."

"Dammit, I said I know what he thinks!"

Tracy stared at Nick with accusing, heartsick eyes.

He sighed. "We'll both go talk with him. We'll explain matters, okay?"

"Okay," she mumbled, gathering Kitty and Toby and waiting while Nick turned the colt loose in the corral.

Together, they headed for the front of the house. Stiffly they walked past the big barn and outbuildings to round the rose bushes. They were almost at the steps when Tracy noticed the sleek late-model Cadillac parked negligently in the drive. It's glossy white hood gleamed in the sunlight. Scattered on the steps were close to a dozen expensively-upholstered suitcases.

Nick drew up short, muttering a word Tracy had never heard him use before the children. Tracy glanced at his face and read a curious mixture of trepidation and hope. "Better late than never," he muttered.

"Who's here?" Tracy asked, unable to resist.

Nick's jaw tightened, his expression tense and thoughtful. "Come see for yourself."

They shooed the children up the steps and into the foyer. There, a scene was being played out Tracy knew would be burned in her memory for a good long time.

Millie hovered in the doorway to the kitchen, wringing her hands and wearing an almost comically polite expression. David was leaning back against the paneled wall, arms crossed, his features schooled into an uncharacteristic, tense mask. His eyes, dark like his brother's, glittered with suppressed masculine ire.

In the middle of the tiled floor was a woman, dressed in a tailored eggshell-colored suit that perfectly matched the car. Her silk blouse beneath was blood red and her nails and lips were tinted the same shade of crimson. Her blond hair was pulled into an elegant French twist.

All three adults turned toward Nick and Tracy as they entered the foyer. David was the first to speak. Surprising Tracy, his tone was rife with sarcasm.

"Ah, good, Nick, you're here. And, Tracy. Fine. You can meet her, now." David pushed away from the wall, holding a mocking hand toward the lovely woman. His eyes gleamed dangerously. "Allow me to introduce you to the returning queen of Roberts Ranch—my lovely wife, Eliza."

Chapter Seven

"Eliza?" Tracy echoed weakly. All at once she felt in need of a chair to rest her trembling legs. And maybe a drink. A stiff one.

"Yes," the woman replied, inclining her head coolly. "And you are?"

"Uh, Tracy. Tracy Wilborough. I..." Her voice trailed off as she tried frantically to find some diplomatic way to tell the woman she'd been hired to care for the other's abandoned children.

David rescued her. "Tracy's the resident nanny. I needed help with the kids after you left, Eliza." David's eyes riveted to Tracy and held her gaze. "She's doing a great job, too. She's a prize."

Uncomfortable, Tracy glanced at Nick, who observed with a maddeningly inscrutable expression. One of his hands rested on Toby's small shoulder as the little boy stared at the strange woman. Aware, always, of Nick's reactions, Tracy saw through his bland expression to the tension beneath. A muscle in his jaw had hardened; his back was ramrod straight. Tracy wondered what to say.

David crossed the few steps separating them and slung an arm about Tracy's shoulders. She was so surprised she almost jumped. "Yep," David went on, giving her a little squeeze, "Tracy's fantastic. Couldn't do without her." He glared at Eliza.

"I see," she returned slowly, giving Tracy a thorough, appraising inspection. Her sky-blue eyes narrowed.

Like a slow awakening, Tracy realized what David was trying to do and wanted to burst out laughing. If it weren't for the gravity of the situation, she might have. Surely an intelligent woman, as Eliza appeared to be, would see through such an obvious ruse.

"Where are Kyle and Kitty?" Eliza asked after an awkward silence.

"Oh, Kitty's right—" Tracy looked around, surprised that the little girl had vanished. She'd been with them when they'd entered the house, hadn't she?

A small movement behind the opened front door caught her eye. Kitty's bright blond head peeked around the edge. Without thinking, Tracy went to her and knelt down. "Kitty, your mommy's home. Come and see her." She held out her arms and Kitty went into them without hesitation.

"Thank you," Eliza said in the most freezing voice Tracy had ever heard, "but I can manage. If you'll please move away?"

Tracy released Kitty and backed up. The little girl clung until Tracy whispered encouragement. Eliza bent, touching Kitty's cheek. "Hello, darling. It's your mother. It's me, Kitty. Give me a hug. I've missed you."

As close as she was, Tracy doubted the others could see what she did—a telltale moisture in Eliza's eyes. She doubted the others would be charitable enough right now to hear the tiny note of desperation in Eliza's voice as she pleaded with the wary three-year-old. "Please, Kitty."

Kitty looked questioningly at Tracy. Tracy gave the girl a small nod and was relieved when Kitty stepped tentatively into her mother's arms. David's bitter voice shattered the reunion.

"So touching," he sneered. Before Tracy could react, he was striding away.

Nick hesitated a moment longer. "I'll get Kyle," he said, following David. Toby trailed after.

That left Tracy and Eliza alone with only Kitty. For the life of her Tracy could think of nothing to say. She blurted the first thing that came to mind. "Will you be staying long?" Instantly she realized her mistake. It made it appear as though Tracy were the hostess of the house instead of Eliza.

"Possibly. Maybe I'll stay for good," Eliza returned stiffly. She straightened, letting her hands fall away from Kitty. "Does that bother you?"

"Oh, no! I mean—that's fine. Um..." Frantic, Tracy searched for a fitting reply. Eyes latching onto the silent little girl before them, Tracy rushed out, "Kitty, why don't you go get a cookie from Millie?" Kitty turned without hesitation to do Tracy's bidding.

At Eliza's indrawn breath and indignant glare, Tracy groaned inwardly. Another mistake.

Tracy decided it was time to clear the air. She clasped her fingers together. "Eliza, I was hired by your husband to care for Kitty and Kyle. I needed the job because I'm widowed with three children of my own. I think I've done a good job with the kids." She hesitated, thinking of Kyle's animosity, and swallowed painfully.

"Anyway, I—I just want you to know—David and I . . . we're not . . ."

"Yes?" the other woman poised on her polished heels, one doubting eyebrow raised.

"Well, we're not involved, if that's the way it seemed."

To Tracy's vast relief, Eliza's eyebrow lowered thoughtfully. She nodded. "I see. Thank you for telling me." With great dignity, she followed Kitty into the kitchen.

Tracy sagged against the wall. She didn't want to be responsible in any way for trouble between David and his wife—even if David had wanted it to appear they were intimate. With a trembling hand, she rubbed her forehead. What a shock! Tracy had never expected Eliza to return. The way the men had talked it seemed she was gone for good.

Straightening, she tried to dismiss the idea that with Eliza's return, her position here would be superfluous. But reality wouldn't be denied. Kitty and Kyle wouldn't need Tracy anymore—not with their mother back. Tracy's time was surely limited. She would be fired, of course. The only question remaining was when? Hours? Days?

At the swinging kitchen doors, Tracy was brought up short by urgent voices.

"But I want to, David. I need to. I missed you all so dreadfully. I—I've been lonely, miserable. Please, David." Eliza's pleading was cut off by David's angry reply.

"It took you a mere four months to realize that, did it?" he raged. "*Four months!* Now you think you can just come waltzing in here and resume where we left off?"

Tracy winced. She backed up a step, loathe to intrude. But the voices were carrying, too loud to ignore.

"No, David, not where we left off." Eliza's voice was calmer now, but held a husky tremor, as if she were trying for control. "I don't want to go back to all the disagreements and arguing. I—I've been getting counselling. I've learned a lot. I feel much better about myself, and I think we can be happy together. If you'll agree to marriage counseling—"

"Marriage counseling! What for? There's not enough marriage left *to* counsel." As she reached the stairs Tracy heard the angry banging of coffee cups on the tiled counter.

"David, I still want to be your wife. And a mother to our children. I understand your bitterness—I..." Eliza's voice trailed off as Tracy finally got out of earshot. She found Toby and Kitty eating cookies upstairs in Kitty's room. Nick was sitting on the bed, watching them. When Tracy entered, he rose and lazily stretched.

"She's something, isn't she?" he offered.

"Uh, yes," Tracy replied. "She's ... something."

Nick patted Toby and shouldered past Tracy without another word. Helpless, Tracy watched him go. Would no one in the household give her any direction for handling this new situation?

As if in answer, she heard a noise down the hall. In the doorway, Tracy glanced out and saw Millie peek from her room. "Millie!" Tracy cried in relief and hurried toward the older woman.

Nick scowled three days later as he caught a glimpse of Tracy walking toward the corral where he was deep into teaching Dan how to whirl a lariat.

"No, not like that son," he corrected gently. He adjusted the stiff rope in the boy's hands and demonstrated the proper circular motion. "That's it. You're gettin' it."

It had been tense since Eliza had made her dramatic return. But he wasn't concerned about his brother's marriage. They would work things out—Eliza had come back, hadn't she? And she'd told a stubborn David she loved him a dozen times in those seventy-two hours. A dozen times in Nick's hearing, anyway. There'd probably been a dozen more in private.

Yep, Eliza was stronger now, able to communicate her needs in a calm, rational manner. It looked like all that counseling had worked.

Those two were the least of Nick's problems. His scowl deepened as he noticed Tracy had reached the corral and was watching her middle child try to rope a fence post. Why'd she have to come out, anyway? It seemed that every time he turned around the woman was under his boot heels.

Nick shook out the lariat and executed a few fancy maneuvers, stepping inside the moving circle and back out again with all the dash of a Mexican vaquero. Next, he prepared to dab a loop on the fence post. The rope whirled overhead, shot out, then slid harmlessly off the post. He cursed under his breath. He was known far and wide as an expert roper—he seldom missed a frisky calf. And never an immovable block of wood! It was *her* fault. He'd been sneaking glances at her, hoping for hints of her thoughts. Had she come to see him? Did she want to be near him?

"Dan, lunch is ready," was all she said, and Nick's disappointment was out of all proportion.

"Aw, Mom, not now. Nick's teaching me to rope a steer! Watch!" With great enthusiasm and little skill, Dan gripped the rope in his small hands. He circled it in wobbly arcs, then let it fly. It landed about ten feet from the post. "Shoot," he said. Dejected, he reeled it in.

"Hey, that's real good," Nick told him. "When I first started roping, I was about your age, you know."

"Really?" Dan asked with small interest. He kept his head down.

"That's right. And at first I couldn't hit the side of a barn! Why, you're better than me already. With some practice you'll probably make me look like a regular amateur."

"Do you think so?" Hopeful, Dan's hazel eyes, so like Tracy's, begged for confirmation.

Nick tousled the boy's hair. "I sure do. We'll practice again soon. Now you mind your mom and go in for lunch. I'll be there in a minute."

Dan ran off and Nick grinned after him. He looked up to see that Tracy hadn't made a move to follow. On her face was an expression of surprised pleasure that warmed him from his hat to his boots.

"Thanks, Nick," she said softly. "Dan gets so little individual attention."

"I've noticed." He closed the distance between them to lean a shoulder on the fence. Today he wouldn't touch her, he told himself. Today, he would just talk. Talking would be safe, wouldn't it?

"—And he really needs it," Tracy was saying. "It's not fair to have to share everything."

Nick nodded, patted his pocket for cigarettes, found one, took it out and struck a match. "I've heard it called 'middle child syndrome.' I've noticed how he repeats everything Brady says and agrees with any old thing that comes out of Kyle's mouth. He's just trying to fit in."

Tracy smiled, her pretty blond hair blowing in the breeze. "He's got to make his own way one day."

"He will. That's partly why I'm teaching him to rope. It'll give him something the others don't have—a small skill to set him apart." He flicked an ash and allowed himself to bask in Tracy's warm approval. Her pert features revealed gratitude, understanding and even a little tenderness.

Her son, of course, was the reason. She recognized that Dan needed attention—male attention—and he was getting it. From Nick. And with that thought Nick knew that he was spending time with the boys partly because he truly cared for them, but partly because they were Tracy's sons.

He squinted at the horizon of white fences and flat verdant pastures. He made no sound to break the silence between them. This was a good place to grow up. Those boys needed a daddy, dammit—he'd told Tracy as much. The fool woman ought to be dating, looking for someone to help raise her brood. She should be dressing up, going to parties. Flirting.

At the image of Tracy all dolled up and hanging on some eager young buck's arm, Nick tensed. The idea was hard to swallow, like the cigarette smoke he was inhaling deep into his lungs.

Impatiently Nick ground the cigarette out. He didn't want another man guiding the boys to adulthood, showing them how to be good men. He didn't want another man to hold Tracy at night.

Angry, Nick dragged his gaze away from the green pastures and grazing cattle to Tracy's face. Her brow was pinched in a pensive frown. She'd been watching the play of emotions on his face, he was sure. And he felt vulnerable, easily read....

It wouldn't do. He cleared his throat. "After you," he said gruffly. He motioned toward the house to cover his embarrassment. "I'm starved for that lunch."

"Okay." She headed for the house, Nick just behind. He enjoyed the unconsciously sensuous swing of her hips, noting she walked without a bit of coquettishness. Tracy was an honest woman. Beautiful and intelligent, he thought. A man could hardly do better. To some, her children might be a drawback. To him, well, he didn't look at things that way.

"You're lucky, you know," he told her. "To have those boys."

Tracy threw a smile over her shoulder. "I know."

"No, I mean it. Dan's going to be some roper. There's talent in those hands."

"Now, Nick, really!" She rolled her eyes.

"Hey, listen!" Nick put a hand on her arm, stopping her in midstride. He had to make her see—he had to show her. "Dan's got a rare skill."

"All right, all right!" Tracy threw up her arms. "He's skilled. What are you trying to say? I couldn't love him any more than I already do."

Nick dropped his gaze. "I know that. I just..." *Just wanted you to know how proud I am of that boy,* he finished mentally. Why it seemed so all-fired important to tell her, he didn't know.

"What's for lunch?" he asked, thrusting his hands in the front pockets of his jeans.

"Your favorite," she said. "Tuna-fish sandwiches."

"Great," he replied. He hated tuna fish.

Millie had counseled Tracy not to rush things with Kyle. She'd told Tracy not to worry about her job, either. But although Tracy trusted Millie about the boy, she didn't think the older woman was right about her position on the ranch. Eliza had been reserved to the point of coldness, although not openly rude. She'd taken a separate room adjoining David's and was spending a lot of time with her children. At least David hadn't continued pretending he and Tracy were involved. She was relieved about that. But she was hardly needed anymore.

For his part, Kyle was thrilled with his mother's return. His relief and joy showed plainly in his eagerness to do every little chore he could think of for Eliza. Tracy saw him fetching her water—plumping pillows for her back—telling her about his summer. The boy was almost pathetically anxious to please.

David, seeing this, attempted to cover the sharpest edges of his resentment toward his wife. But his moods were dark and uncommunicative—such a contrast from his previously preoccupied, but good-natured personality.

Kitty passively accepted her mother's return, but showed a lack of real affection for her, preferring to seek out Tracy and Toby as soon as Eliza's attention was diverted.

Tracy just felt sad. Although there was no friendliness from Eliza, there was courtesy, and Tracy's sharp eye saw through Eliza's cool exterior to the pain and remorse beneath. Telltale brightness in Eliza's eyes, a pleading note in her voice, deeply drawn breaths sounding like a sighs— none of them were lost on Tracy. The woman was hurting, and with the empathy of a mother who loved her children, Tracy understood.

In the kitchen snapping fresh green beans for Millie's dinner, Tracy was feeling depressed when Nick stopped in for a soda and casually dropped a bomb: in two week's time he would be riding in a local rodeo. Tracy had been too stunned to say anything. She went numbly through the motions of preparing the vegetables and setting the table.

"Nothing official," he explained to everyone over dinner. "Rodeo season is mostly over. This one's put on by a nearby ranch—the Lazy L. The boys over there are pretty keen on competition. I'm only riding at the Lazy L in preparation for the state championships."

Tracy tried to hide her misery. "And you're..." she began in a thin voice, then ran out of air. She cleared her throat and tried again. "You're going to enter the competition for saddle-bronc riding?"

Looking faintly surprised, Nick said, "Well, sure. It's what I do."

Tracy dropped her gaze to her plate and pushed her beans around.

"Can we watch, Uncle Nick?" Kyle begged, almost jumping in his chair.

"Yeah, can we?" Brady said around a mouthful of rice.

"Are the horses gonna buck real hard?" Dan asked eagerly.

All eyes went to Dan. It was one of the few times he'd offered an original thought. In the surprised silence, the boy began to blush.

Nick hurried to fill the gap. "Sure, Dan, those nags at the Lazy L are gonna buck and twist like crazy. But they won't get rid of me. Not if you come to give me luck."

The other kids started yelling in excitement, all but Dan, who just sat grinning at Nick with a smile as big as Montana.

Tracy produced a weak smile.

Nick met her gaze steadily. "You'll come, won't you, Trace? To, uh, care for the boys, of course."

Visions of violent bucking...furious horses...and dangerous folly struck her, nearly choking off her air supply. She saw Nick flying off a horse...the sharp hooves trampling him...blood.

Unbidden, a horrible image leaped into her mind of Craig's lifeless body lying in that coffin at the mortuary. All because of his reckless, careless sport. She shuddered and commanded her thoughts to stop.

"Trace?" Nick prompted.

"I can't," she whispered.

"Aw, Mom, come on," wailed Brady. "If you don't go then we can't!"

Tracy saw Kyle direct a hopeful glance at his mother, but she was shaking her head. "You know I don't like rodeos, Kyle. I'm sorry," Eliza said.

Slowly, Kyle turned to Tracy. On his boyish face she saw glimpses of his previous anger and frustration. Since Eliza's return, Tracy thought he'd been less cool toward her—as if he realized she'd never been the woman for his father, after all. Now, his expression changed to uncertainty. "Please?" he asked her.

"I—I don't think..." As she tried to let him down easily, her eye caught the still posture of her middle son. Dan's hazel eyes were riveted on her face. He was barely breathing—waiting, hoping.

In that moment she knew she couldn't disappoint Dan. He'd begun blossoming here—and a good deal of credit went to his idol, Nick.

"All right," she said, resigned. "If Nick rides in the rodeo, we'll go."

The kids cheered, and she felt Nick's grin warm on her cheeks. But she couldn't meet his gaze. She didn't want to be a hypocrite and let him think she approved.

She didn't think anyone noticed when she quietly excused herself from the table and slipped into the family room. There, she paused, restless. She found herself at the front door, yanking on a light windbreaker.

Outside, Tracy hugged her elbows against the new coolness of the evening. Fall was almost here, the boys had already started school. She wondered unhappily if she would have to leave soon.

Shivering, she walked fast, trying to drum some heat into her chilled limbs. But even as she strode along the gravel walkway toward a far pasture, she knew the attempt would be futile. Because the cold came from within.

It had been stupid to imagine her discussions with Nick might convince him to rethink his life-style. She'd been silly, thinking the strength of her arguments—the logic, the practicality, the *wisdom* would sway him. She'd been a fool.

Reaching the end of the walkway several hundred yards from the house, she stopped at last and braced a weary shoulder on the fence. From the pasture the wind carried smells of hay and cattle and manure and dust. She inhaled gratefully, liking the earthy scents. Would she have to move back to the city and content herself with city odors of gasoline exhaust and industrial fumes?

She would have to leave here sometime, that was becoming certain. Even supposing her services as nanny were still wanted, she couldn't stand to watch Nick leave for each rodeo, terrified he would be maimed or killed. She knew that now.

Startling her, the sound of boots crunching on the gravel broke into her thoughts. She whirled to find Nick bearing down on her, and he didn't look happy. "What the hell are you doing?" he demanded. "It's cold out here."

Tracy straightened and lifted her chin. "I needed some time alone. Time to think."

"To think about what?" His eyes narrowed.

Averting her gaze to the placid sight of grazing Herefords in the distance, she wrapped her arms tighter about her middle. "I'd prefer to keep my thoughts to myself."

"That'll be a first," Nick muttered.

Tracy glared at him. "You're right. I have been too opinionated—with you. I should never have presumed to tell you how to live your life." *It didn't do any good, anyway,* she added silently.

"Right. But you have, ever since the day you set foot on this ranch."

Eyes back on the white-and-red coats of the cattle, Tracy was horrified by the knot of pain rising in her chest threatening to lodge in her throat. Behind her eyelids, tears burned. Lifting her chin a notch higher, she forced out a hoarse, "Sorry."

"That's good," Nick returned. "But all of a sudden I've got a perverse desire to know what put that burr under your saddle. The way you started frowning over dinner and then jumped up from the table got me wondering." He paused. "Well?"

Tracy drew a painful breath. "Nick, just go away, all right? I don't want to talk." She hunched a shoulder away from him.

"No need to play games, Tracy. Because I already know. It's the rodeo, isn't it?"

Tracy was mute, staring at the horizon.

When Nick moved around, forcing her to face him, her temper broke.

"Yes!" she told him. "It's that damn rodeo. You know how I feel about it. But you'll go ahead and ride anyway. You'll put yourself in needless danger—and the boys will all think you're terrific. They'll idolize you even more—maybe even want to become rodeo stars like you! It's...upsetting! It's...terrible!" She felt her throat working, felt the sting of tears slide from the corners of her eyes. Angrily, she wiped them. "There. You asked and I told you. Satisfied?"

Nick's face had closed during her tirade. His skin looked stretched taut over his harsh features. At his sides his hands were balled into fists. "No!" he roared. "I'm *dis*satisfied! And I've had enough of your meddling in my life—telling me what to do—how to live. Let me tell you something, missy. What I do is none of your business. I've never kowtowed to a woman before and I sure as hell won't start now."

He advanced on her and Tracy took a step back, stunned by the strength of his response. She could do nothing but listen, trapped by the intensity in Nick's furious eyes.

He jabbed a finger toward her chest. "I'm telling you plain out—your womanly ways and your little pouts don't hold any water with me. I'll do as I please. Got it?"

Tracy nodded, feeling frozen through and through. She stared at him. "God, you're cruel," she whispered.

"Yeah? Well, maybe if you pulled your head out of the sand you'd see that I'm not cruel. Just honest."

With a kind of morbid curiosity, Tracy wondered aloud, "Do you treat all women this way? Haven't you ever been in love?"

Nick snorted. "Love's for fools."

"You—you don't believe in love?"

"I didn't say that. Let me tell you something, honey. A man and a woman don't *fall* in love. They *dig* their way into it."

"What an awful attitude."

He shrugged—a proud man, confident in his philosophy. "It's true. Every time I've felt more than was seemly for a woman, I simply lit out—before any damage was done."

Trembling now, Tracy's fingers were unsteady as she laced them together. A consuming anger shook her. "You coward! And you accuse me of running from life? Why, you've been doing a fine job of it yourself. Tell me," she continued before he could answer, "How many hearts have you broken over the years?"

"None, dammit! I just told you—"

"You told me you 'lit out' as you put it, when *you* felt more than lust for a woman. But what about them? Did you ever consider *their* feelings? Maybe, just maybe, one or two was already in love with you before you so conveniently broke it off."

"I doubt it," he said, but she detected uncertainty in his eyes and knew she'd hit home. Like a dark cloud, a short silence hung between them. Tracy was shocked to realize she'd suddenly lost the desire to press her advantage.

It didn't matter, really, she told herself with unaccustomed listlessness, because the two of them would never have a real relationship. He wouldn't allow it. *She* wouldn't allow it.

She turned away, disheartened, hurting, chilled.

Nick hesitated a moment longer. Then she heard his muttered, "Aw, hell," as he pivoted and stomped back toward the house.

Tracy shivered, colder than she'd ever been in her life.

Chapter Eight

Rodeo day dawned bright and miserably clear. As Tracy reluctantly shepherded Kyle, Brady and Dan into the double-cabbed truck, leaving the youngest two children in Eliza's care, she struggled to suppress her foreboding.

Once roundup had begun, tension on the ranch was thick. The work made for long days for them all. Nick and David had worked closely with the cow boss, and each morning they would saddle up to gather calves for branding. Sometimes Tracy watched in the dawn's misty light as Nick's big gray bucked out his morning excitement. Then, Nick would ride off with the others, whooping it up.

Tracy had helped Millie with the cooking since extra hands were hired on. The children couldn't get home from school fast enough. The afternoons found them hanging on to the fence rails to watch the procedures of branding and innoculating, asking dozens of questions and generally getting in everyone's way.

Eliza spent her days either sequestered in her room or caring for her children. Kitty remained aloof from her mother and her behavior saddened Tracy because it so obviously distressed Eliza. The nights Eliza spent in private, apparently unsatisfying conversations with David.

Toward Nick, Tracy had maintained a cool reserve, his command that she quit meddling in his life still stinging fresh in her ears. In the past ten days Nick had made several obvious attempts at making up to her, but Tracy couldn't forget about the upcoming rodeo. Then finally roundup ended.

It was silly, this dread welling up within her, she thought. Nick had performed in hundreds of rodeos and lived to tell about them. Why would today be any different?

The drive to the Lazy L went quickly. Occasionally she caught Kyle's shy glances at her. Since his mother's return, his animosity had evaporated. And now Tracy figured he was ashamed of treating her so coldly, but like any awkward nine-year-old he hadn't the least idea how to apologize.

As they bumped down the driveway lined by a white split-rail fence housing sleepy Herefords, she realized the crowd of perhaps two hundred was far larger than she'd imagined.

"All this for a local rodeo?" she wondered aloud.

"There's fierce competition between the ranches around here," Nick explained.

"I see," she replied numbly. "And you're a real fierce competitor, huh?"

"The fiercest." Nick arched an arrogant eyebrow, refusing to be baited.

He pulled over and the kids spilled out. As he jammed the transmission into park, in his expression Tracy recognized eager excitement. It was the challenge he loved, she reminded herself stoically. Danger was only part of that challenge. Nick hopped out and Tracy exited the truck with considerably less enthusiasm.

Nick came around the hood and took her arm. "Here we are," he announced heartily.

"Don't remind me," she muttered. She glanced around at milling cowhands in dusty buckskins and jangling spurs, children hanging on the area rails, and a red-and-blue striped canvas tent that shaded the concession stand.

But Nick was hauling her over to a tall man with a full head of white hair and loud voice who held court with several men. She recognized them as competitors in the rodeo, not because she knew them but by their shared air of machismo. That, and Nick's identical mood of anticipation and reserve. She tried not to grimace.

"Ben Laramie," Nick announced when the elder man greeted him, "I give you Tracy Wilborough. Tracy, meet Ben, owner of this sorry spread. Don't let his smooth manner and wily ways take you in. The old goat is a womanizer from way back."

"Never had any complaints, yet." Ben gave Nick a broad grin and whacked Nick across the shoulder blades, then pivoted to give Tracy a thorough going-over. She could well imagine women's attraction to the man with his direct sky-blue eyes and appreciative manner. Before he could speak, Nick pulled the boys close.

"These hombres are two of Tracy's. You already know Kyle, here, David's boy," he added, and Tracy wondered at the trace of pride in his voice as he introduced them all. Ben Laramie shook hands with the boys, solemnly welcoming them before he lifted his gaze again to her. She said hello and caught a speculative gleam in his eyes going from her to her kids to Nick.

"You're all welcome here at the Lazy L," he boomed, pumping her hand. In a loud aside to Nick, he muttered, "Classy, Nick, very classy. No wonder you're grinnin' like a skunk eatin' yellow jackets!"

Tracy relaxed, feeling her first genuine smile of the day pull at her lips. Nick shrugged, saying nothing, but his smile was wide. "Trace," he suggested, "why don't you get the boys some popcorn while Ben and I look over the stock?" He gestured with his chin toward the far paddock where horses milled nervously.

"Okay," she said, "we'll catch up with you later. Nice to meet you, Mr. Laramie."

"Ben," the man shouted over his shoulder. He and Nick were already heading toward the paddock and she bit her lip, watching them go. If she didn't think much about Nick atop one of the skittish animals, she would somehow hang on to her good humor, she told herself. But everywhere she looked reminders stabbed at her.

Behind the chutes cowboys limbered up—stretching neck and back muscles. Some, the calf ropers, threw practice ropes around sawhorse steers. Over the loudspeaker came strains of Willie Nelson's "Mamas, Don't Let Your Babies Grow Up to Be Cowboys" and the air was heavy with smells of dust and horse and seasoned leather, as well as popcorn and hot dogs.

Kyle tugged her toward a huge steer standing in a box pen with a sign overhead proclaiming, The Biggest Steer in Montana, and listing his impressive height and weight. Tracy smiled. She knew that by including her, Kyle was, in his way, apologizing. She dutifully admired the animal. "It's a big cow, all right," she remarked.

"Steer," Kyle chided good-naturedly. "Not a cow." He raced off after Brady.

Nick rejoined her, sliding a casual arm about her waist. "Want a hot dog?" he asked, already shelling out the money to a vendor. While they ate, he introduced her to his many friends and appeared determined that she would have a good time. Tracy was touched as well as bewildered. The way he blew hot and cold on her would confuse anyone!

Dan, jogging ahead as they crossed the arena, paused before two men practicing roping. He watched shyly, until Tracy gently encouraged him to try his hand.

"Can I?" Dan asked a grizzled cowhand whose scuffed leather chaps had seen better days.

"Sure thing." The cowboy handed over the stiff lariat and Dan carefully tested its weight in his hands. Mindful of his lessons, he concentrated on whirling the rope overhead in concentric circles before unleashing it to land in a perfect arc over the sawhorse.

Tracy cheered and Kyle and Brady whooped congratulations. The cowboy clapped Dan on the back as he took the lariat, but it was the near-to-busting pride on her son's face that gave Tracy the most pleasure. She saw Dan search for Nick.

Nick grinned, giving Dan a thumbs-up. "Didn't I say you were good?"

As Nick's gaze met hers, Tracy had a fierce wish that he wouldn't ride today. Maybe—just maybe he would change his mind. Maybe he'd decide she was right about the folly of it all. If she asked him to just watch with her perhaps he would be content with that.

He took her hand and Tracy allowed hope to soar. She pushed aside any doubts of being unreasonable. All the problems between them seemed to melt away as their gazes held. Suddenly Tracy realized that because of Nick's efforts she was enjoying herself. It was surprising, given the horrible anticipation she'd had to endure these past few days. But he was a compelling, attractive man, all male, and for today at least he was devoting himself to her. Her fingers tightened on his. "Nick," she began. "How about if you don't ride—"

Just then Ben Laramie's voice over the PA system called the riders to the chutes and Nick squeezed her hand. "Gotta go," he said, and headed off with the other riders. Heart sinking, Tracy let her shoulders droop. *Of course he was going to ride,* she chastized herself. Of course he was. It was what he did best, wasn't it? The path he'd chosen for himself? The main pleasure in his life?

The boys pulled an unprotesting Tracy toward a row of metal bleachers erected for the rodeo. They settled somewhere in the center, squeezed between a middle-aged woman sporting a beehive hairdo and eating cotton candy that looked amazingly like her hair and a trio of giggling teenage girls.

Dully, Tracy listened to Ben's good-natured voice as he introduced the different events. She barely noticed the calf roping begin—but managed a wan smile when Ben praised the winner, remarking, "That cutting horse could turn on a dime and offer change."

The events passed in an unreal blur until Ben announced the saddle-bronc competition. Then, everything about the arena became crystal clear as Tracy's senses went on overload.

Like a vivid dream, the colors of the crowd became unnaturally bright. The first man up had a red kerchief tied at a jaunty angle around his tanned throat. Tracy stared at the bright bit of crimson as the man was jolted to and fro by the bucking horse. The cowboy was thrown. He got up and limped away.

The next rider wore a brilliant yellow shirt with mother-of-pearl buttons and large sweat rings under his armpits. He was thrown, too, but came up laughing good-naturedly.

Midday sun glinted off the sloping top of the nearby tent until Tracy had to look away or risk a headache. Her jaw began to ache from the strain of her clamped teeth; she felt her own sweat rings forming.

"Ladies and gentleman," echoed Ben's voice, "now we've got a special treat for y'all—a local boy I've known since he was knee high to a grasshopper. Fresh from the circuit, he's here to show off what he's learned over the years. On top of Greased Lightning today... Nick Roberts!"

From her vantage across the arena, Tracy saw Nick's fingers flex on the rope rein, gaining exactly the right purchase. Barely breathing, she could see, even at this distance, the ropy muscles in his thighs contract about the big bay's middle. At last he gave a curt nod to the chute attendant and the door flew open. Bursting from the opening came an explosion of horse and rider.

The boys' shouts were lost in the roar of the crowd. Tracy half stood, caught by the incredible dramatic power of the twisting, bucking horse and by Nick's concentrated skill in working him. His blunted spurs raked with precise rhythm from the horse's shoulders back to his rump—coinciding with each buck as if in a choreographed dance. The hat held in Nick's right hand fanned gracefully up and down.

Puffs of arena dust churned under the bay's thrashing hooves. The horse grunted. He struggled with the unwanted weight and irritating bucking strap, and the scene itself imprinted on Tracy's senses. More tense than she'd ever been in her life, she could almost feel the heaving horse beneath her.

Time crept umercifully slow as Tracy held her breath. Only eight seconds, she told herself, ticking them off on her fingertips. Eight seconds was such a short period of time. He would last that long, she assured herself, counting down.

She had two fingers left: her ring finger and her pinkie, when Nick was thrown.

One minute he was looking good, in control, working the horse, the next the horse took a sudden crab hop and spun to the left, unseating his rider with ridiculous ease. For a long second Nick seemed to simply hang in the air. The next he was falling sideways, crashing with sickening force into one of the arena's rails, his head splintering the wood.

Through a flurry of dust, Tracy peered, horrified. She screamed, a small thin wail lost in the crowd's collective gasp.

"My God! Let me through. Please, *let me through*!" she demanded, stumbling from the bleachers and racing for Nick. With her elbows and knees and hands she forced her way. But it was like swimming against a strong current. For every two steps forward it seemed as if the crowd pushed her back one.

Hot, blinding tears spilled down her cheeks, and frustrated, she scrubbed them away with the back of her hand. She wanted to scream again, this time in frustration. Didn't these people know she had to get to him? Didn't they *understand*?

At last she reached him. The rodeo doctor was already gently probing Nick's neck and head.

Dropping to her knees in the dust, Tracy took one look at Nick's still face, at the bright blood seeping from a gash across his forehead, and felt her sick panic reach hysterical proportions.

"Don't you die on me, Nick Roberts," she whispered frantically, hovering over him. Her hands were shaking. "I can't take it, do you hear me? I can't take it!"

"He ain't gonna die, miss," the balding doctor told her impatiently but not unkindly. "Move back, please, so I can get a better look at the wound."

Tracy stared at him. "He won't die?"

The doctor inspected the gash, then gave her a brief smile. "It'd take more than a little toss off ol' Greased Lightning to kill Nick Roberts. His ornery hide's a mite too thick to go so easy." While he talked he withdrew a stethoscope from a leather case and listened to Nick's chest. Then he folded the instrument and muttered, "Hell, Saint Peter probably wouldn't even take 'im."

Nick stirred and opened his eyes. He tried to get up but the doctor pressed him down. "Stay put, you old cuss. You got your bell rung good, so now you're gonna have to pay for it."

"Trace?" Nick said weakly.

Tracy scooped up his big dusty hand in both of her own and held it to her chest. "You'll be all right," she told him over and over, assuring herself more than him. "You're okay. You're fine."

She hardly paid attention when a gurney arrived and Nick was lifted onto it and carried to an ambulance. The attendants were forced to work around her because she refused to let go of Nick's hand. She looked up only when the boys pressed near. On Kyle's and Brady's faces she read grave concern and quickly reassured them. But Dan was valiantly fighting tears.

It was Dan's reaction that convinced her to let Nick go. She herded the boys back to the truck, got the keys from the glove compartment, wrestled the engine to life and roared after the flashing red light of the ambulance.

Ben Laramie showed up at the hospital some two hours later to offer his support. Tracy had purchased vending-machine sandwiches for the boys and coffee for herself while they waited for the final verdict on Nick's condition. The hospital doctor wanted an X-ray of Nick's skull, and perhaps a few other tests. Ben arrived near the end of their wait.

"Sorry about Nick," he told Tracy, settling onto a chair beside her in the waiting room. "But don't you worry, he'll survive. He's tough."

Tracy grimaced over her coffee. "So I've gathered. I just called David and he seemed so unconcerned I couldn't believe it. Then he explained that Nick's been in and out of hosptials with injuries like this for most of his adult life."

"Yep," Ben returned, nodding. "Rodeo circuit's a rough career." He frowned at the three boys. "I hope none of you want to take it up."

They all shook their heads, eyes wide.

"That's good." Ben placed his elbows to his knees and smiled at Tracy. "It's probably good for these boys to see the downside of the life as well as the glamour. Too many kids think it's all fun and games."

"That's right," Tracy said, her spirits lightening a fraction. If there was a bright side to Nick's accident, his demonstrating to the boys the real danger of his job could be invaluable. She shook her head. "If only Nick would heed the downside himself, I, for one, would be happy."

His chin on a palm, Ben studied her. "Would you?'"

Tracy fought a blush.

"Sorry. Didn't mean to embarrass you. And I've got an idea you're just what Nick needs. A woman who really cares for a man is worth all the cattle in Montana."

"Thanks—I think." Tracy gave him a wry smile.

"Mrs. Wilborough?" The hospital doctor, a harried man who wore his lab coat inside out, stopped before Tracy. He flipped through several papers on a clipboard.

"Yes?"

"Nick's going to be just fine. He's got multiple contusions, a deep laceration on the forehead that I've sutured closed—took fourteen stitches—and a slight concussion. He'll need several days of bed rest. I'd like him to spend the night here for observation, but frankly, we can't strap him to the bed."

"Strap him...?" Tracy repeated, at a loss. At Ben's hearty laughter she faced him, confused.

"Never could keep that boy down." Ben gave Tracy's shoulder a squeeze and sauntered down the hallway toward the parking lot. "You take care of him, honey." He paused at the door, giving another loud guffaw. "If you can."

"Can we see him?" Tracy asked.

The doctor frowned. "Room 348. Maybe you can talk some sense into him. I couldn't. He really ought to—"

The boys raced off, Tracy hard on their heels, before the doctor had even finished.

Nick recuperated nicely. He insisted on being driven home the same day, but agreed to go to bed once he'd gotten there. On seeing Nick sitting up in the hospital bed, giving the nurses hell and yelling for his boots, Tracy felt a rush of relief so profound she'd had to get off her shaking limbs and take a chair.

She was in love with Old Stone Face.

The boys crowded around him, clambered onto the bed, asked to see his wound. But Tracy simply slumped in her chair, drinking in the sight of the man she loved, happy he was alive and well—or close to it. For those few moments it hadn't mattered that he didn't requite her love. That's when she knew her feelings had grown to such proportions. The fact that she cared more for his safety than anything else told her the unfortunate truth.

Tracy had little sleep that night and the following day she had the greatest shock yet when Nick called her into his bedroom and made an announcement.

He sat, propped against pale blue sheets and sporting a white bandage on his head. His faded chambray shirt was rumpled and unbuttoned. At his side were a cast-off breakfast tray with cold coffee and toast crumbs, several wrinkled magazines and an ashtray brim full of cigarette butts. Millie was just leaving the room, shaking her head and muttering something about Nick's being an "ungrateful coyote."

"Hi," he said to Tracy, his eyes lighting when she entered. He shoved aside the tray and patted the bed beside him. "Come in. Have a seat."

Tracy prudently took the bentwood chair. It wouldn't do to let him know how badly she would like to get beneath the covers with him. "Hi," she returned, her thoughts making her shy.

"Uh, I've got something to say," he began, scratching the itchy growth of beard on his jaw. "I just don't know how to say it."

Tracy smiled. "Straight out usually works best for me."

"Right." He hesitated another moment, seeming to gather his thoughts. Then he fixed her with an intent stare, watching her closely. "I'm quitting, Trace. I'm not rodeoing anymore."

"What do you mean?" she returned warily. "No more rodeos this month? This year?"

"You know what I mean, honey," Nick said softly. "I'm quitting. For good. I've been laying here in this bed fighting with myself about the decision. But I've pretty much known for the past year that my career was winding down. It's time to get on with my life." He produced a lopsided grin.

"But," she breathed, "why, Nick?"

"You may not believe this, but at twenty-eight, I'm considered something of an old timer on the circuit. Most of the boys riding today are nineteen or twenty. In the mornings I ache, Tracy. My bones are getting brittle, my muscles have taken a beating for too long."

"But . . . you've known all that at least a couple of years, haven't you? Why decide to stop now?" Perversely, Tracy felt the need to get to the bottom of his reasons.

Nick shrugged, lifting a hand to his bandage. "I've been lucky, getting off with only a few broken bones, a few injuries. But lately I've been thinking that I ought to quit before there's any serious damage." He paused. "Also . . . you've opened my eyes about some things."

"Like what?" she prodded.

"Like the worry my family has to endure. When the boys and you rushed into my hospital room yesterday—all frightened, pale faces—I remembered what you said before. You claimed I should consider those that care about me." He shrugged again, plucking at the blue comforter. "Hell, my brother and Millie, even Kyle has begged me, over the years, to give it up. I just didn't listen. Didn't want to hear." He met her gaze levelly. "You changed all that. Even though I fought you, too, I began realizing you were right."

"That's good," Tracy replied mechanically. She drew in a deep breath. She wondered how this change in Nick's life would affect hers. The last barrier to her reasons for hoping for a life with him had crumbled. While he insisted on competing, she could maintain her anger with him—despite her other feelings.

But now there were no shields. Only the major fact that Nick didn't love her. He didn't want to get involved. He'd made it clear, many times, that he wouldn't tie himself to one woman.

Nick went on. "When we got to the Lazy L, I tried to show you a good time. I—I wanted you to have fun like most folks who go to a rodeo."

"I did have fun, Nick. Until you were thrown."

"I know. I could see the fear in your eyes all day. In fact, your fear affected me. I was worrying about you—worrying about me—and it divided my attention when I rode. I wasn't any good out there."

Tracy gasped. "You mean... it was my fault? If I hadn't been there you wouldn't have fallen?"

"No!" Nick cut an impatient hand through the air. "Don't be ridiculous. Woman, can't you understand what I'm trying to tell you?"

Tracy shook her head slowly. Her fingers were cold; she curled them together in her lap. "I guess not."

"I'm saying I care about you. I didn't want to—hell, I still don't. But it's too late. You're under my skin now." He glared at her. "I can't stop thinking about you."

"You don't look too happy about it!" Warring equally in her was the desire to throw herself into his arms and the urge to throttle him. He'd said he cared for her, but he obviously resented it.

"I'm *not* happy about it," he thundered. "But I guess I'll get used to it."

"You make me sound as if I'm some sort of awful medicine you just *have* to swallow." She got to her feet and wondered if perhaps his decision to quit the circuit was really at the root of his anger. "Maybe you shouldn't give up rodeoing, Nick," she said, thinking fast. "Not if it means such sacrifice in another area of your life."

Nick's epithet was short and succinct. "Are you saying now you *don't* want me to quit?" His eyes went heavenward. "That's just like a woman."

"Haven't you heard?" Tracy returned, stung, her anger growing apace with his. She'd never had a man furiously yell his affection for her. "It's a woman's prerogative to change her mind."

"Why?" Nick stared at her, his expression stony.

Tracy moved to the foot of the bed. She knew Nick was asking why she'd changed her mind. But something was wrong. This avowal of love, if that's what it was, didn't follow the caring, passionate tone she'd imagined and hoped for. Spurred by a suspicion, Tracy decided to push him.

She swallowed hard, hoping she would lose the gamble. "Rodeo is at the very core of your self-image, isn't it? You see yourself as a saddle-bronc rider first, don't you, and then as a rancher?"

"I guess."

"And—and you identify yourself that way. Will you be content to be just another rancher and not Nick Roberts, rodeo star?"

"I won't *be* just another rancher. I'll truly be a part of Roberts Ranch and making it successful."

"People will call you a hasbeen, you know."

"No."

"Yes, they will," she insisted. "It's bound to happen. It will someday, whenever that day comes, that you're forced to quit."

Losing patience, Nick gritted his teeth. "What are you getting at Tracy? Make your point."

Tracy retreated another foot away. With a sinking heart she knew she was on to him now. He wasn't ready to settle down. Maybe he *thought* he was, but she knew better. If he quit now he would be looking over his shoulder all his life. Wistful. Regretful. And later maybe resentful.

She fastened her gaze on the foot of the bed. "I'm saying... maybe you should give the matter more thought. It's too big a decision to make in one day."

"But I told you—"

"I've got to see to the kids, Nick. I'm going now." She was at the door.

"Wait, dammit! I'm talking to you!"

"I'll have to leave the ranch soon, anyway. Even though David and Eliza haven't asked me to go yet, I'm sure my presence here is superfluous."

"But..."

"Yes?" She fiddled with the doorknob, acutely aware that although Nick had at last admitted to some feeling for her, he had made no mention of a future for them. Yet he looked suddenly lost. A niggling doubt assailed her. Had she been wrong? "What is it, Nick?" she asked softly, hopefully.

"I don't want you to take the boys away. I've invested in them, you know. My time, my energy. They admire me—like you said, remember? I'm their hero. And I really lo—like them."

"I know. But I can't very well live here without a job, can I?" She looked at him steadily. When his gaze fell, her throat tightened into a knot of pain. No, she hadn't been wrong. She'd been dead right. With numb fingers she closed the door behind her and went to look for Toby.

Chapter Nine

Nick stuck by his decision. He told her so in terse tones the next night after dinner and then stalked away. He was angry—obviously she hadn't reacted the way he wanted when he dropped that bomb about quitting. But what had he expected? she asked herself, tossing and turning in bed. Did he think she would just throw herself into his arms?

Tracy snorted and rolled over onto her side. Lord knew, she'd wanted to at the time. But her suspicion that Nick had acted hastily had grown into certainty. She'd seen his tell-tale frown as he'd read a *Sports Illustrated* article about bronc riders. At the breakfast table Nick had made an appearance, moving slowly and still bandaged. He picked up the magazine along with a steaming cup of coffee. Under his breath he cursed all through the reading, forgetting his cooling coffee, and ended by slamming the magazine onto the table and storming away.

Tracy understood when she scanned the article. It featured glowing references to Billie Roy Jenkins, one of the men Nick considered a rival, and said very little about Nick himself. His decision to quit was already eating at him, Tracy realized unhappily. Now, only pride compelled him to stick it out.

"Tracy?" The bedroom flooded with light.

She bolted up in bed, one hand going to clutch the edges of her granny nightgown as Nick stepped into the room. With her other hand she rubbed her eyes and blinked in the sudden light.

"Sorry to wake you. There's something I've been wanting to say." He stood just inside the room, all long-legged, lean-hipped confidence. He held his thumbs hooked negligently in the front pockets of his jeans. He wasn't bothering to keep his voice low, she noted through her surprise. A man who'd come to seduce a woman in the middle of the night would whisper, wouldn't he?

"Yes? What is it?" Her heart was still beating double time.

"Just this—I listened when you harped at me about the rodeo's dangers—even when I thought you were wrong—even when I didn't want to hear. But I gave your words credence. I want the same courtesy from you."

Tracy stared at him. She noted his booted toe tapped almost nervously and the muscles in his jaw clenched tight. "You came in here at two in the morning to tell me—"

"It couldn't wait. I want to know when you're going to stop comparing me with your husabnd."

Tracy's jaw dropped. "Compar—"

"What makes you so gosh-darned sure I'm as reckless as him? I've got a lot of years behind me as a professional. I know what I'm doing."

"Yes, well—"

"It appears to me your husband was pretty amateurish, if your description of him is reliable. He got killed because he pushed himself past his capabilities, didn't know his limitations."

"I know, but—"

"I'm different. I *know* my limitations. That's why I'm quitting! The grind's no good for me anymore. I'm tired of it. But I've managed to keep in one piece for ten years." The reference to Craig's lack of expertise was obvious. Tracy began to get mad.

"You're so sure of yourself, aren't you?" She got to her knees on the bed. "You didn't even know Craig."

"Right," he returned, coming closer. "But you did. And now you know me. I just don't want you getting the two of us confused." He jabbed at her collar bone with one tanned finger. "So remember, I'm a different man and ours is a different situation."

He stepped back, a hand on the doorknob. "Think about it. And while you're at it think about what you're going to do in the future." At her sudden frown he said, "I have a right to say that—you've asked me the same often enough."

Tracy's silence was mutinous.

"Until you accept some facts, nothing will work out," he finished vaguely. "Nothing worthwhile, anyway." He held her gaze for a long moment, flicked off the light and closed the door. She heard his footsteps echoing down the hall, then heard the soft hush of his bedroom door closing.

Frustrated, Tracy shook her head. She'd known Nick wasn't like other men: she'd had firsthand experience with his eccentricities. But this beat all. And such vague statements. *Nothing will work out.* What was that supposed to mean?

Settling back in bed, she pulled the heavy quilt up to her neck and folded her hands over her stomach. That man surely had fulfilled her original premonition; he'd certainly complicated her life.

Why should she consider anything he said? Hadn't he caused her more trouble than a pack of renegade coyotes?

After several fruitless minutes of trying to maintain righteous anger, Tracy gave in. He really hadn't awakened her; she'd been thinking about him, anyway. Even if he was wrong about her, she couldn't be upset about his concern.

He might be right about one thing, though. Her future. After all—it wasn't just hers, but her boys' lives for which she was responsible. A conscientious parent would map out goals, plan college educations for her children, provide a stable home.

All she'd thought about lately was herself and one unpredictable cowboy.

Tracy closed her eyes tiredly, weariness enfolding her in waves. Tomorrow, she promised herself, tomorrow she would give the matter some thought. As she drifted toward sleep, the suggestion of Nick's comments became almost posthypnotic. She loved the man, didn't she? When one loved a person, one should consider his ideas. Maybe he wasn't one-hundred-percent wrong, she allowed. Maybe only ninety percent.

She sighed, imagining his strong arms around her, his warm lips on hers, his voice whispering words of praise and love. Feeling magnanimous now, she sighed again and charitably lowered the figure all the down way to eight-five.

Last night he'd accused her of comparing him to Craig, she recalled, frowning in concentration. While Kitty and Toby crayoned nearby, she sat quietly in the sun and gathered nerve to ask herself some harsh questions, no matter how much they hurt. She was determined to keep her promise to herself and examine Nick's accusations. Though why it should hurt baffled her.

Had she transposed Craig's amateurish recklessness onto Nick?

A few short months ago she'd leaped at the position of nanny. A life free of worry about rent and food money sounded so wonderful. It was true that she seldom thought of Craig now—their good times and the bad had faded in the face of Nicholas Roberts's vibrant personality.

But the question had to be asked: Had she been wrong to uproot her boys and run from her bad memories?

Tracy's glance fell on Toby as he crouched happily next to Kitty. They were in the small yard off the kitchen enjoying the last bit of outdoor warmth before winter set in. To the casual observer, Toby's and Kitty's blond heads, bent close together and similar in shade, could mark them brother and sister. The two had grown to love each other as siblings.

Tracy thought of Dan's eagerness to show her his school projects each afternoon and of his newly acquired self-confidence, due in large part to Nick's attention. She thought of Brady's satisfied smile, reflecting new pride in his horsemanship.

Aside from missing their grandparents, each of her boys had displayed positive reactions to their move to Montana. So what had Nick meant? If he'd referred to her refusal to accept his profession, then, yes, she *had* resisted adopting the silly hero-worshipping posture of the others.

But if he wasn't referring to that, she didn't know what he meant. Millie, David and even Eliza had made her and her children welcome and had given them all time and space to properly recover from Craig's passing.

Tracy smiled sadly. Even if she would have to leave Roberts Ranch now, she knew she'd done the right thing.

As she moved a bit apart from the kids, she felt her motivations for everything she'd done were probably sound. In addition, in unexpected ways, she'd matured a little. Today she'd recognized some fundamental needs in herself and discovered most of them had been met here in Montana.

But was heartbreak a fair payment for peace of mind?

A few moments later Tracy was mildly shocked when Eliza sought her out. The woman had become cordial, but still not actually friendly. She greeted the children, oohed and ahed over their artwork and then approached Tracy where she sat across the yard. "Can we—that is—do you mind if I sit with you?"

"Of course not." Tracy patted the bench seat of the picnic table beside her.

The other woman cleared her throat, then adjusted her perfectly ironed silk collar. "I, ah, wanted to ask your advice about a problem I've been having." Eliza's voice was no louder than a whisper and her gaze flicked over the children.

"Oh." Nonplussed, Tracy blinked. "Well, you don't have to whisper, no one can hear us out here."

"Yes, they can!" Eliza whispered again, her eyes going again over Toby and Kitty.

"You mean you don't want *them* to hear us?" Tracy waved a hand toward the kids. What kind of tale-bearing could a pair of tots be capable of?

"It's about Kitty," Eliza explained, even more softly. Her azure gaze locked on the face of her little girl with the bright intensity of a mountain lake. "I—I've made some errors in judgment. I'm afraid I've lost—" She took a gulping breath and broke into silent sobs. Her slender shoulders heaved.

For an awkward moment Tracy waited in silence. Then she wrapped an arm about Eliza's shoulder and squeezed. "I understand." She'd seen Eliza's efforts at winning back her young daughter. She'd seen the attempts at hugging and kissing, the cajoling with toys and candy that Eliza had tried. And she'd seen Kitty's resistance. Eliza's endeavors had held an underlying desperation the little girl was sure to sense.

Eliza made an effort to get herself under control. "Everything I do for her only earns me a blank stare or a polite thank-you. She seems to prefer you—I don't mind her affection for you, you understand," Eliza rushed to explain. "But I'm her mother! She won't let me hug her—she won't touch me," she wailed quietly. "My little girl doesn't love me anymore!"

"Eliza," Tracy began as kindly as she could. "There's anger in Kitty." Both women turned to look at the girl. She was humming, her rosebud mouth turned up in an angelic smile as she scrubbed a butter-yellow crayon over the paper.

Looking confused, Eliza asked, "Anger?"

"Didn't you know that when you left, your children would feel abandoned?" Tracy asked as kindly as she could.

"Oh, no! I love my children! I wasn't leaving them—I had to get help. My self-esteem was fading, my marriage crumbling—don't you see I—"

"But children can't comprehend the *why* of situations. All they knew was that their mommy had left and she might never come back. I think this is Kitty's way of dealing with that. She's protecting herself from more pain."

"God, I've been such a fool." Eliza dropped her face into her hands. "Have I lost Kitty's love forever?"

"Of course not," Tracy assured her, hoping she was right. "She does need you. And she needs reassurance—and time."

Eliza heaved a shaky breath. "I'll try."

"I'm glad. I think—"

"Mommy?" Kitty was there, in front of Eliza.

Eliza looked up. Tears streaked down her cheeks; her usually neat chignon slipping unheaded onto her neck. She stuffed her hands into her lap. "Yes, darling?"

"Why are you crying, Mommy?" The little girl lifted one small finger and touched a tear on her mother's cheek.

Glancing uncertainly at Tracy, Eliza sought an encouraging nod, and getting it, she ventured, "Because, darling, I'm so sad. You remember when Mommy left before, for such a long time?"

The little girl nodded.

"Well, I'm worried you might think I'll leave again. But I won't. Not ever. I missed you so, Kitty, and I love you. I'd never, never go away without you again. Do you believe me?"

"Yes. But..."

Eliza waited and Kitty scratched her nose. "Go on. What?"

Eyes downcast now, Kitty used her toe to prod a tiny sow bug making imperceptible progress across the yard. "When you go, Mommy, you don't say goodbye."

"I don't say goodbye?" Eliza repeated in a puzzled tone. "What do you mean?"

"When you go. You don't say goodbye," Kitty said again.

Eliza glanced helplessly at Tracy.

Tracy had to swallow away the tightness in her throat. The woman had made some major mistakes, and now she was paying for them. *Please don't let me make such errors,* she prayed. "To a three-year-old, four months is an eternity. Saying goodbye somehow always assures my kids I'll be back soon. Maybe Kitty feels the same way."

Eliza swallowed.

As if she understood perfectly, Kitty smiled, then announced, "I like teddy bears," only it came out, "I *yike* teddy bears." She leaned against her mother's knee, one of those affectionate gestures children perform unconsciously. Tracy knew Eliza was savoring the simple act. "Will you buy me a teddy bear?" Kitty asked.

"I'll buy you a hundred ted—" Eliza caught Tracy's quick frown and stopped herself. "I'll buy you one *small* teddy bear," she amended. "And we'll have a tea party with him, okay?"

"Okay. Toady gets one, too," Kitty demanded, scrambling away to get her colors.

The children bent once again over their crayoning, and Eliza sighed, turning back to Tracy. She offered huskily, "I'm sorry I've been cold toward you. I've no excuse except maybe jealousy. When I got here and found you taking over with my children—and then doing a good job of it—"

"It's okay." A wonderful sense of well-being filled Tracy with a joy that almost erased the pain in her heart. She thought for a moment, then felt bold enough to ask, "What about David?"

Some of the joy faded from the other's face. "Well, he isn't yelling at me anymore, at any rate. And I think I'm making progress in talking him into seeing a marriage counselor with me."

"That's great!"

"We'll see. I'm just not certain..."

Tracy patted the other woman on the arm, grateful for their new camaraderie. "It's obvious that he still loves you."

"Do you think so?" Desperate hope tinged Eliza's voice.

"I sure do. Anybody can see how he stares at you with calf eyes when he thinks you're not looking."

"Oh, Tracy!" Eliza's smile was as wide as the Missouri River. She gave Tracy a quick hug of appreciation. "You're just saying that!" Clearly she was begging for confirmation.

"Nope. I mean it." Tracy returned Eliza's smile, then noticed David appear in the kitchen doorway that led to the yard. She noted how his wary gaze flickered over his wife and settled on Tracy.

"Can I speak with you, Tracy?" His voice was polite, and Tracy noted how he kept his gaze scrupulously off Eliza.

"Of course." She rose and followed David into his office. He'd never before asked for an audience with her. Panic seized her throat when she realized that he might be planning to give her the ax. She wasn't ready to leave Roberts Ranch, a voice screamed inwardly. None of her problems were resolved yet!

"Sit down." David offered her the maroon-striped chair she'd occupied on arrival only two months before. This time, a good deal more apprehensive, she gingerly placed her bottom on the front few inches and clung to the edge with stiff fingers.

He half sat on the corner of his desk and leaned one casual forearm on his knee. A thoughtful frown furrowed his brows.

"You don't have to ask me," Tracy blurted.

"I don't?" His brows rose.

"No." She dropped her eyes to study a broken fingernail. "I'll go."

A broad grin spread over his face. "Great! That's good news."

Tracy's head snapped up; she tried not to cringe at his relieved tone. "Wh—when?"

"Saturday," he returned brightly. He got off the desk and went around it to stand before her. "The boys will be tickled."

"Tickled?" She said weakly. It was not a word she would have chosen.

"Yeah! I know you don't like rodeos, Tracy, but the Playday is nothing like the real thing. It's mostly for kids, but some adults compete, too."

Lost, Tracy stared at him, gradually realizing they were talking about two different things. Hoping for a clue, she repeated, "A playday?"

"Right. It'll be great—there'll be equestrian events, goat tying, egg races, all sorts of fun things." His smile grew. "I'm glad you've agreed to go. The boys were afraid to ask you themselves. They thought you might say no. Especially Dan."

She sighed, releasing her pent-in worries. In comparison to losing her job, a kiddie rodeo didn't seem half as bad. She was surprised at the gush of relief flooding her limbs. She loosened her grip on the chair and raised a wry eyebrow. "Am I wrong in supposing there'll be a roping event?"

"How'd you guess?" He grinned. "Listen, the events Brady and Dan want to enter really aren't dangerous. And it'll be good for them. Fun."

She hesitated a moment longer. "Fun? I guess so."

"The boys will be ecstatic."

"I know I am," she answered in exaggerated tones and they laughed together. She left the room wondering if she'd lost her mind, allowing her precious children to compete in a rodeo.

In the cool weekend dawn Tracy was rudely awakened by the excited too-loud whispering of Kyle, Brady and Dan right outside her door. Her response was to burrow deeper into the blissful warmth of her quilt.

The boys were having none of it. Tracy could hear their hushed voices coming closer to her bed. "Should we wake her?" Kyle wondered, somewhere in the vicinity of her left ear, and Dan whispered back, "Naw, let 'er sleep. We can go downstairs and practice roping and stuff." The muffled sound of Brady cuffing his brother and his caustic, "*You're* the only roper here, Dan. *You* go practice. Kyle and me're riding," made Tracy take pity at last and smile at them from sleepy eyes.

"I'm awake, I'm awake. Is something special happening today that I should know about?" she inquired innocently.

The three fell into shocked silence. They exchanged glances, then Brady ventured, "Didn't David talk to you the other day, Mom? He said you told him we could go."

"Go where?" she asked, teasing.

"Aw, Mom." Dan grinned, punching her arm. "You know. The Playday Rodeo."

Tracy sat up in bed and rubbed at her offended arm. "If you're going to beat up on me, I don't know if I can go along with it." She spoiled the effect of her threat by smiling at the hopeful faces and earned herself a hearty tackle by three growing boys.

"Say yes, Mom," Brady demanded, bouncing the air from her lungs. Kyle had her legs shackled and Dan added his fifty-odd pounds on top of her to Kyle's. "Say yes!"

"Whumph," she said under their wriggling weight.

"She said yes," Kyle yelled in triumph. They all jumped off, cheering, and raced from the room as if afraid she would change her mind.

Tracy chuckled and swung her legs over the side of the bed. She rubbed at her forehead and wondered again if she'd lost her mind—going to a rodeo, even one for children. It was hard to believe. But she was, and she decided to try and enjoy it, come hell or high water.

She put on faded form-fitting jeans, a feminine Western-cut shirt of bright peach and a hand-tooled leather belt. She frowned at her tennis shoes and shrugged.

Downstairs the boys were filling the dining room with echoing shouts of excitement, and curious, Tracy led a yawning Kitty and Toby toward the noise. Millie stood in the kitchen doorway, smiling and watching. In her hands she held a pitcher of fresh-squeezed orange juice.

Nick was holding court, the boys bounding around him like new colts kicking up their heels in spring sunshine. Nick's head was still swathed with the white bandage, and he held his left arm close to his body, as if favoring his shoulder again. She knew he'd landed on it when he'd been thrown.

Over the boys' heads he met Tracy's eyes. "Okay, buckaroos, Tracy's here now so you can have your presents." From the table he lifted packages and handed one to each. Even Toby and Kitty got smaller ones.

"What's this?" Tracy asked. "It's not Christmas."

"Nope. But they'll be needing these today."

"But how'd you—you've been in bed."

"I went out day before yesterday when you were picking the kids up at school," he explained.

She nodded, realizing she couldn't possibly know all his comings and goings. She'd never even been able to find out where he went all those times he'd disappeared, either.

In a frenzy, packages were opened to reveal child-sized cowboy hats with braided leather bands. Each was a different shade, so it could be easily identified by the owner. Toby's small as it was, still dwarfed his little head, but he didn't mind, making snuffling cow noises and funny high whinnies like he'd heard coming from far paddocks. Kitty caressed her soft ivory-colored hat with its Indian-feather headband and started twirling like a prima ballerina in a new tutu.

For Tracy, the sight of her boys so thrilled with their "real-live cowboyhats" as Brady's awed voice proclaimed them, it was a poignant scene. Once again she was possessed of warring urges to kiss Nick in gratitude and scream at him in fury. Didn't he know he was only going to make their leave taking that much harder?

The kids raced out of the room in search of a mirror, and Millie murmured only, "Land sakes!" before disappearing into the kitchen. They were alone. Nick indicated a package still left on the table. "That one's for you."

Tracy stared at it but made no move. More than anything she wanted Nick's gift but was afraid to touch the package. Gift giving should be reserved for people who really cared for each other, she thought frantically. He was killing her, she decided, biting her lip. The man had no clue of how wild she was for him.

"Well? What in Sam Hill are you waiting for?" He gave an impatient nod toward the package.

Still she hesitated.

"Go on." He picked it up and thrust it into her hands, then jammed both his into his back pockets. "Open it."

She felt a reluctant smile forming at the edges of her mouth. What woman could resist the charm of a little boy coming to the surface in a grown man?

She opened the box and found a pair of the most elegant snakeskin boots she'd ever seen. The low heel was buffed to a high gloss, the toe smartly pointed. The calf-length tops were embroidered in a design of fancy curlicues. The pattern was stitched with dark gray thread that contrasted beautifully with the softer gray of the leather. She checked the size. Six. Perfect.

"Well, come on, woman. Try them on!" Nick pushed her into a chair and bent to pull off her tennis shoes and ease the boots onto her feet. Above him, Tracy watched his ministrations with a tight throat. She noted his hair, ground into a whorl on the side where the bandage forced it away from its natural growth. Her eyes wandered over the deeply tanned grooves bracketing his mouth. She marveled at the length and richness of his lashes. In his expression she read endearing eagerness to please.

He did care for her, he did! If only he would realize it, she thought shakily.

"There. Stand up," he directed, eyes on the boots. "I told the cobbler exactly what I wanted. They look all right to me, but then I'm pretty hard to please." He grinned at her.

"That's an understatement," she muttered, and instantly regretted it when a flicker of uncertainty washed over his features.

Tracy launched herself into his arms. "Oh, Nick, I'm sorry. I love the boots, they're beautiful. And they fit so well. I...well, I...just thank you. Thank you so much."

Awkwardly he patted her back and cleared his throat. "Don't mention it. It's nothing."

"Nothing! handmade boots—and snakeskin! Nick Roberts, I'm not such a city girl I don't know these must have cost a fortune."

He shrugged, stepping out of her embrace, clearly embarrassed. The hands went back into his pockets. "Money's for spending, isn't it?"

With a valiant effort Tracy kept her emotions in control. "Thank you for the hats, too. The boys are pleased."

Nick shrugged again, turning away to clear up the empty boxes. Gruffly he said, "I should've gotten them for the kids a long time ago. Been busy, that's all."

"Yes."

"They live on a ranch now," he informed her unnecessarily. "They gotta have hats. And you need boots." He glowered at her as if daring her to contradict him.

Unfortunately, his comments only reminded her that if she had to leave, her boys wouldn't need the hats nor she the boots. She kept her thoughts to herself, caring for Nick too much to spoil his joy in the giving. The kids picked that moment to come tumbling back into the room, Kyle shouting, "Let's go! Time to leave!"

Dan and Brady grabbed her hands and towed her toward the door. "Hold on," she said. "We don't have to leave yet, do we?"

"Maw, we gotta go *now*. Come on, David's in the car already. He's waiting!" Dan pulled harder on her arm.

"Okay, okay," she said, growing exasperated. The tugs on her arms were firm and just this side of painful. Her boys were getting older, stronger. They'd grown some during the summer here. They were healthier now than ever before. For some inexplicable reason it made her sad. "Just a minute. Where's Eliza?"

"In the car," Brady supplied.

Tracy held back. "And Toby and Kitty?"

"With Millie."

"Let me get my sweatshirt, then. You run ahead. Tell David I'll be right there." Tracy shooshed them out, hoping she wouldn't have to meet Nick's eyes. She didn't think she could take much more heartache. Hurriedly, she gathered her extra clothing from the back of a chair and headed for the door.

But Nick was behind her. "Wait." His loud voice snapped over her head like a crack of summer thunder.

Tracy refused to turn around. She wanted only to escape. Around him, her feelings for him were too emotionally charged. "Yes?"

"We have to talk."

She shrugged. Whatever he wanted to discuss certainly wouldn't be what *she* wanted. "All right. Go ahead."

He took her elbow and forced her to face him. "Did you think about what I said the other night?"

"Sure did," she drawled back, hoping her sarcastic tone sufficiently hid her misery.

"And?"

"And..." What the hell. *Tell him, you chicken!* Thin and wavering, her voice got stronger as she went along. "I agree that I have unfairly compared you and my husband. I agree I've been avoiding—no, *escaping* unnecessary excitement in my life, and that you personify—" she swallowed hard "—excitement. But I came to the conclusion that it really doesn't matter to you, Nick. You needn't concern yourself." At last she met his gaze squarely.

"Well, I *am* concerned." With his chin thrust forward, he spread his arms wide. "So, what are you going to do about this problem?" He pointed a lean finger toward the door. "Those boys need a daddy."

"Fine!" she shouted back, suddenly angry herself. Well? Her eyes dared him. Was he going to propose? An interminable moment dragged by during which Nick failed to say anything at all. Tracy wanted to scream and cry and curl into a miserable ball, but she forced herself to bluff it out. With jerky movements, she gestured in the direction of the stables. "Behind which barn are you keeping all the eligible men?"

He said nothing, he just kept glaring at her.

In the tense silence Tracy's anger dissipated as quickly as it had come. She sighed, feeling defeated. Nick saw the problem, all right. He just didn't see *himself* as the solution.

With a kind of apathetic acceptance, she knew the issue she'd been afraid of facing was resolved. She would leave the ranch. Tomorrow. She would let the boys have their fun at the rodeo, and in the morning she'd pack their belongings into her ancient station wagon and head out.

Tracy looked at the man she loved through bleak eyes. "I'll be moving in the morning. We'll go into Red Lodge.

Or maybe down to Bozeman. I'll get a job there." Another part of her was mildly curious at the surprised look on Nick's face. But she quickly smashed any fanciful notion she might have had and with shaking hands tied the sweatshirt around her neck.

He was staring at her. "You'll do *what*?"

"I have to, Nick. This...situation between us...well, the tension is becoming unbearable." She drew in a deep, deep breath that lifted her rib cage. "I find my work with the children is affected, I can't concentrate on anything anymore—I'm not happy here now."

"Are you saying I make you unhappy?" he demanded.

For a long minute Tracy considered the question. But all that came to mind was a great longing for him and the bliss of sheltering in the haven of his arms. But she couldn't tell him this. Not now. So she said the only thing he would understand. "I'm afraid so."

"That's just great."

"Mom! We're waiting!" Dan's pleading call came from the front yard, through the opened front door.

"I think," she began, hanging on to the knotted ends of her sweatshirt as if they were the reins of a runaway horse, "I think maybe you'd better not come to the Playday."

Nick's frown deepened. "Why not?"

"It's going to be hard enough on the boys," she answered simply. "They'll be looking to you for approval, and after today you'll no longer be part of their lives. Let's just make the break as painless as possible. I'll make your excuses, okay?"

He thrust a hand through his hair behind the bandage, leaving it mussed. She thought she saw a fine trembling in his fingers, but quickly decided she'd been wrong. Oh, Nick cared about her. The problem was, he didn't care *enough*.

His dark eyebrows pinched together, almost forming a straight line across his forehead, and the weathered brackets beside his mouth looked as stiff and unyielding as leather. He half turned away from her. "If that's what you want," he said gruffly.

She hesitated a moment longer, but in the silence between them she heard only the rumble of the truck's engine kicking to life and the kids calling to her. With one last glance at Nick's profile, she walked out. There was nothing left to say.

Chapter Ten

On Tracy's first visit to town, the day she'd arrived in Montana, she hadn't seen much of the lively Western village nestled at the foot of Red Lodge Mountain. And today her lackluster mood discouraged her from joining the boys as they craned out the car windows. Authentic taverns lined dusty Main Street with names like Willow Creek Saloon and Big Sam's Cafeteria.

David pulled up to the rodeo grounds and the boys burst from the big truck with wild Indian war whoops. After pushing the keys into his pocket, David came around to take Eliza's elbow. Tracy saw Eliza's brilliant smile as she gazed into her husband's face, and Tracy was happy to see his return grin. He tucked Eliza's hand into the crook of his arm and started after the boys. Sighing, Tracy thought, well *good*. It was high time those two worked out their differences.

But her happiness for them couldn't banish her depression. Even the weather matched her mood; gray, vague clouds drifted aimlessly overhead and a dry, swirling wind swept up from the ground to whip her hair into her eyes with a painful sting. She reached into the truck for her borrowed coat and sank into its warmth. By chance she caught Eliza's concerned glance dart over her and tried to smile reassuringly, but the pall that hung over the day seemed to hang over her spirit, as well.

She was glad Toby and Kitty had stayed home with Millie. She didn't feel like fussing over anyone. As they headed for the arena, she noticed cowboys with dirty boots and well-worn jeans riding low on their hips, some had arms around pretty gals dressed in their best fiesta finery of denim skirts and fringed vests. And children were everywhere. From five-year-olds to teenagers, they were gathering to compete, each hoping his special skill would win a status-giving blue ribbon.

Rodeo personnel had tied bright helium balloons onto the concession booths, Tracy noted, but in the heavy wind they batted each other and flew at an angle rather than straight up.

With a sudden loss of interest, Tracy shut her eyes against the image of Nick's closed face as she'd left the house.

Nick was a fighter. He would fight to the death for anything or anyone he loved; Tracy knew this instinctively. If he'd felt strongly enough—she forced her thoughts to a halt, he'd let her walk away without even token resistance.

"Everything okay?" Eliza's low voice was close to her ear and Tracy turned to see compassion in the other woman's eyes.

"Sure!" Tracy forced out.

"Sure." Eliza nodded knowingly. She took Tracy's arm and waved David and the kids off toward the entry table. Tracy found herself guided to a set of folding chairs by a concealing row of hedges. "Want to talk about him?" Eliza asked.

Tracy didn't bother evading the issue. She sighed, rested her elbows on her knees and her forehead on one palm. "I—I'm afraid he's a lost cause, for me anyway. He—he doesn't love me."

Folding her hands in her lap, Eliza studied Tracy. "Nick hasn't discussed your relationship with me, and I haven't asked. I've respected your privacy. But I think you might want to hear a few things now." An arched eyebrow asked if she should go on.

Tracy nodded.

"I can't say Nick is definitely in love with you, Tracy. But I can tell you I've known that man for many years and I've never seen him act this way before."

"What way?" Tracy asked guardedly.

Eliza's long nails glinted in a sudden patch of sunlight as she gestured with her hands. "Oh, distracted. Preoccupied. The way his eyes follow your every move. The way he's been mooning over you."

"Mooning?" Tracy sat up.

"I think so."

"But he hasn't mentioned anything to you about how he feels for me?"

The other shook her head. "I'm sorry."

Tracy slunk down into her original position. Nothing had changed, although Eliza meant well. The patch of sunlight disappeared as the eddying clouds again took over. She'd better tell Eliza the truth. Dully, she sighed. "I haven't told the boys yet, but we'll be leaving the ranch tomorrow."

"But you can't leave!"

Tracy offered a wan smile. "Your husband hired me because he needed help with the kids. You're back now, Eliza. Kyle and Kitty have you. And Nick certainly doesn't want me. I wonder if he can truly care for any woman."

"Tracy," Eliza said urgently. "I don't want to see you get hurt. But don't give up yet. Nick's a good man. He's responsible for helping save my marriage."

Tracy tried to hide her surprise but Eliza was too sharp-eyed. "It's true. Last night David and I sat up talking. He—he's agreed to go with me and meet with a psychologist I've been going to. Last night we—" her color rose "—er, well, we made up."

Tracy touched her arm. "That's great. But what does Nick have to do with it?"

"Nick's the one who kept urging me to get counseling—even when I wasn't living at home anymore. He picked me up several times in the last few months and drove me to the therapist's office. He waited for me in the lobby and would take me out to lunch or dinner afterward." Eliza's eyes softened. "Oh, Tracy, he was wonderful. We had long talks and I was able to come to grips with my problems. I'm grateful to have such a caring brother-in-law. Most wouldn't be so understanding."

There was silence between them while Tracy thought about Eliza's words. The picture Eliza painted of Nick added a dimension to the man Tracy had seen little of, although she'd caught glimpses of his kindness in his treatment of her boys.

It was so like Nick not to call attention to his caring for others. Eliza's revelation only made Tracy's heartache worse.

Then, like a blast of the near-gale winds buffeting them, the realization came: *that* was where Nick had been all those times he'd disappeared. And it explained Millie's uncharacteristic reticence. She'd known where he was all along.

To Tracy's surprise she was able to say calmly, "You've given me a lot to think about. And I'm glad you and David have worked out your problems."

"They're far from worked out, Tracy." Eliza laughed. "But I have high hopes. You see, the major contention between us was over my career. I need more stimulation than I can get just staying home." Eliza suddenly grew intense, leaning closer. "I want to work, Tracy. I love my interior-decorating career—and I'm good at it. David's beginning to realize this and accept it. So, you see, I want you to stay on—keep taking care of the kids. And to be my friend. You will, won't you?"

The temptation was almost too great. Tracy fought it...and won. Just barely. "I'm sorry. More than anything I want to stay on the ranch. I—I love it there." Tracy was horrified when her voice cracked. It took tremendous effort to steady it. "Please understand. I can't."

Eliza pondered, studying Tracy's face. "All right. For now. But I didn't give up on my marriage, I fought for it and I'm making headway. You and Nick—I believe in you both, as well."

Tracy worked up a grateful smile for Eliza's vote of confidence. But in her heart all was as bleak and dull as a moonless night.

As the boys each proudly presented her with ribbons they'd won, Tracy managed to convey the proper interest and pleasure. But inside she was a mass of confusion.

She was restless. She couldn't stop thinking about Nick's guarded, tight expression as she'd left that morning. Yet he hadn't lifted a hand to stop her. Actions spoke louder than words, didn't they?

Her inner turmoil only increased as time passed. Around her revolved people and animals and colorful banners, buffeted by the high winds. They added to her jumbled thoughts.

She didn't want to give up on Nick. She wanted him. She wanted a life with him. A home. Apple pie. Family. But what could she do? Impatient and frustrated by her inability to resolve anything, she felt her fists clenching at her sides.

Probably he was bored by her—the colorless little widow woman with the even temper and simple, homebody tastes.

At the thought, Tracy grew even more unhappy. She'd never done anything truly exciting in her whole life, and Nick practically ate danger for breakfast!

A man like him wouldn't be truly interested in someone who was afraid of her own shadow.

Tracy's eye fell on a twelve-year-old boy adjusting the cinch of his horse's saddle in preparation for the calf-roping event. Some of the entrants were adults—out just for the pleasure, but most were children. The boy gave the latigo a yank and patted his horse's neck. He chattered happily with friends; they tossed out dares and challenges to each other.

Tracy frowned. Even these kids, her own included, weren't afraid of a little vigorous fun.

Nick, she decided insightfully, had been right about her.

He knew her so well—she saw that now. But she hadn't ever really understood *him*. Now she would be leaving with the mystery of why he'd felt compelled to compete still unsolved. The loose end rankled.

When it came, the idea was like a bolt out of the endless gray Montana sky. Why not? If he could do it, then so could she. Before sound judgment or reason could intrude upon her decision, Tracy went into action.

A teenage girl, a small brunette with a long ponytail, who Tracy had learned was pulling out of the competition because her chestnut horse had stepped on her foot, sat glumly watching the others. Her foot was elevated with an ice bag on top. Tracy sidled up to her. Thank heavens she had rapport with children, she thought, initiating a conversation with the girl and managing, somehow, to convince her to loan Tracy her horse.

"I guess it'll be all right," the girl said, still dubious. "I'm glad *somebody* will be able to ride Miriah since *I* can't." She frowned at her swollen foot. "But my mare's a little nervous, you know, 'cause of the crowds and excitement. She didn't mean to step on me, and I should've taken off my sandals and put on my boots before leading her out of the trailer. You sure you've done this before?"

"Absolutely," Tracy answered truthfully. Well, she *had* barrel raced before. Many times on her parent's farm and sometimes in friendly races with the neighbor kids. She would be rusty, of course, but she knew she could do it! "I'll take good care of Miriah," she assured the girl. With that she headed for the entry table and offered her name for competition. The man handed over a number, which she pinned onto her back.

The family was at the hot-pretzel stand, getting a snack before the other competitions began, so Tracy was able to make arrangements without their knowledge. Then she took up a post at the arena rails and began studying the riders' horsemanship for pointers. Anticipation tingled through her limbs.

Entering the rodeo was bound to give her invaluable insight into Nick's motivations. Aside from that, it would be fun. Of course, it wasn't bronc riding, even she wasn't so stupid to attempt that. But *she* would feel the power of the horse beneath her. *She* would hear the roar of approving crowds and *she* would know the exhilaration of competing—woman and beast against the clock!

At last she would be able to experience rodeo from the inside, and not just on the fringes. *At last* she would see what drove Nick. Who was this man she only partly knew? What was this thing he loved that she only partly understood?

Today, she would have her answer. She would be able to satisfy her questions once and for all. Sadly it would have no impact on her relationship with Nick. They *had* no relationship. Tracy drew in a quick, hard breath. Then she tamped down all emotions save an eagerness to get on with the adventure.

Feeling giddily crazy and carefree, she barely heard Dan approach and point at the number on her back. His mouth full of pretzel and mustard, he asked "Mom, what's *that* for?"

Tracy surprised him by picking him up and whirling around. "It's for me!" She set him down, bent close and asked in a conspiratorial whisper, "Did you know your old ma has always secretly wanted to barrel race?"

"No," came Dan's muffled answer. He was still so surprised he forgot to chew.

"Well, it's true. I'm going to have some fun today. I'm going to ride that pretty chestnut over there." She pointed to Miriah, who was tied to a nearby hitching post. "And I'm going to *race* like the wind around those barrels." She threw her arms wide on the word *race*, then got so close to Dan their noses touched. "You gonna watch?" she whispered with a grin.

Round-eyed, Dan backed up a pace, then another. He didn't answer, apparently so befuddled by his mother's unusual behavior he was speechless. At last he gulped down the hunk of dough in his mouth and shot over to where Brady and Kyle were admiring their ribbons.

Tracy rolled her eyes heavenward. He didn't understand. None of them would. She was a *competitor* now. A contender. Tracy giggled, covering her mouth with her hand. So what if she felt a little hysterical? All this nervous tension would help her concentrate on the ride. That's all that mattered now.

"Mom!" Brady careened up to her, trailing Kyle and Dan like the streamers of a kite. The kids crowded around, hopping and yelling. Brady asked excitedly, "Are you really gonna enter the barrel racing? You don't have a horse!"

"Yeah," Kyle concurred. "You don't!"

"I sure do," Tracy told him, indicating the mare.

"That's rad!" Kyle pronounced. "I bet you're gonna fly around the ring." He flung his arm toward the arena, then stopped short. "But you're *old*. You'll be the oldest one out there." He grinned at her, clearly proud of his deduction.

Tracy grimaced.

"Yeah," Brady said, puffing out his chest. "But my mom can do it. She's cool."

"Cool," Dan agreed.

Just then David walked up. "Tracy, you can't be serious!" His eyes moved to her number and back to her resolute expression. Eliza stood behind her husband. She frowned but didn't interfere.

"I most certainly am," Tracy returned stubbornly.

There was a shocked silence that David broke by muttering, "She's lost her marbles." He straightened, then in an aside to Eliza said, "I'd better call him. Maybe he can talk sense into her."

Tracy ignored them. The first competitor had begun and she was intent on cataloging every detail of the rider's technique. She felt free and unfettered and beautifully detached from constraints. She was going to do it. Today. She'd made up her mind and no one could stop her.

"What the hell did you say?" Nick bellowed into the phone. David's tinny-sounding voice came laced with static over the telephone wire.

"You'd best hightail it over here, and quick. The woman's gone mad! Maybe you can reach her. We tried. She—she's acting weird. I can't explain it. You better just come."

Nick slammed down the receiver with such force it was a wonder the molded plastic didn't shatter. He wished it had, he told himself furiously, storming for the door and pausing only long enough to yank his sheepskin jacket off the hall coat tree. He jammed his hat down over the bandage.

Millie stood in the kitchen doorway, a broom held idly in her hand. "You going after her?"

"Damn straight I'm going after her. She doesn't know what she's getting into. She could get hurt. *Killed!*" he swore under his breath.

"But why are *you* going?" Millie asked, an irritating smile playing around the corners of her mouth.

"Why?" he thundered, one tan hand pausing on the doorknob. "Why do you think?"

"Oh, I know why, Nick. The question is—do you?"

Nick glared at her and she glared right back. His muffled epithet was still echoing in the hallway as the door slammed.

Behind the wheel of his pickup, Nick drove like a furious, snorting bull intent on running down a rodeo clown. He hunched over the wheel and stomped so hard on the accelerator he heard the scrape of the pedal's steel against the floorboards. "Damn fool woman," he muttered, cursing the miles as they sped past them.

Tracy gripped the braided leather rein in the shaking fingers of her left hand as she'd seen the others do. With her right, she grabbed hold of the saddle horn so tightly her fingers turned white. Anticipation, that was all, she told herself.

Miriah tossed her head and blew hard. She pranced sideways, fighting the bridle, and Tracy tried to speak soothingly to her, but the mare wasn't to be calmed. Oh, no. Not today. Not when the blasted horse knew she had a chance to get the bit between her teeth and run like Man O' War.

With a concentrated effort Tracy managed to bring the horse under control and she felt her exhilaration build. Slowly, a sense of power seeped into her senses, flowed through her. She was controlling this big animal, bending it to her wishes. It was thrilling!

When Miriah quieted, Tracy took a few seconds to scan the crowd. She was surprised but gratified to find so many pairs of eyes already turned toward her. Eager expressions, expectant faces waited...all for her!

Was this how Nick felt, during competition? Of course it was. She was experiencing the very same emotions and pride he'd tried to tell her about! Pleased with the idea, she grinned. *I'm onstage,* she sang inwardly.

But the rodeo officials were unaccountably delaying her turn, and as the minutes dragged by Miriah became agitated again. Suddenly, the horse half reared, nearly unseating her rider. Miriah's flank bumped into a wooden post of the arena and just missed crushing Tracy's leg. Tracy gasped, struggling both to regain her stirrups and hold the reins.

The near accident only strengthened her resolve. She crooned to Miriah in the same low monotone she'd heard Nick use. Stroking the horse's neck, she forced herself to ease the nervous grip of her legs about the mare.

There was no fear, only expectancy and a strong desire to discover for herself what all the excitement was about.

But she already knew, a small voice whispered. Without even racing yet she knew what had held Nick in thrall all these years. And she understood.

By the time Nick reached the outskirts of town he'd worked himself into a fine lather. His facial muscles felt drawn and wooden from the black scowl that had settled there.

The pickup's grumbling tires gave up blacktop for gravel as he slammed to a halt. Because of the crowds, he had to park a quarter of a mile or so from the arena. He cursed that fact, too. The wind shot up and grabbed great shovelfuls of dirt and tossed them angrily in the air, so that when Nick got out of the truck he could hardly see.

But it didn't matter. He knew the grounds so well he could get here blindfolded. He'd practically cut his teeth inside those very arena rails! And he'd seen a lot of people hurt over the years right here, as well. He, himself had been hurt there a time or two. His breath came a little faster.

But Tracy wouldn't be, not if he could help it. The idea of seeing her thrown off whatever skittish nag she'd managed to borrow sent chilled vibrations down his spine and quickened his already hurried steps.

Fear had been a close companion of Nick's over the years. He'd known it most days riding the rodeo, and known it intimately. But mostly, he'd been able to conquer its paralyzing effects and extract only the productive, adrenaline-producing qualities that had served him well. In some ways fear had been a friend.

But not today. Images of Tracy suffering any of the injuries he'd experienced made his throat tight and sore. Barrel racing was dangerous! In his mind he saw her knees slam into the heavy metal barrels as she rounded them, saw her lean a scant inch too far to the left when her horse was turning right. He saw her fall, get her foot caught in the stirrup and get dragged beneath the horse's sharp hooves.

His breath coming in rasps now, Nick approached the arena at a dead run. Scanning the crowd, he recognized Tracy's honey-blond hair as she struggled to control a high-strung chestnut. Before he could get around the arena, he heard the announcer calling her name.

"Stop!"

Even through her excitement, even over the crowd's hum, Tracy heard Nick's bellowed order. She couldn't help the rush of pure relief that sung through her and left her weak at the sight of the tall cowboy.

He came to a halt at her horse's shoulder and glared at her from under his Stetson with the darkest scowl Tracy had ever seen.

"Have you gone crazy?" he yelled. He reached out to capture Miriah's bridle and steady her. "What the *hell* do you think you're doing?"

In spite of Tracy's relief that he'd thought to come to her, the sheer arrogance in Nick's tone gave her pause. Her chin lifted a notch. "I—I'm going to barrel race. Kindly let go of the bridle. My turn is up."

"No way," he bit out. "Just do as you're told and get off that horse."

"Do as I'm told?" Tracy echoed. The mare, nerves already stretched taut, danced and worried the bit and Tracy had to wrestle with the reins. "I'm afraid you have no right to order me around, Nick. Now, please. Move."

The gatekeeper was waiting with one hand on his hip and the other on the starting whistle. Tracy heard the announcer call her name a second time. "Ma'am?" the attendant said, "Are you ready?"

"She's not riding," Nick tossed back over his shoulder.

"Yes, she is—uh, yes, I am," Tracy insisted, trying to wrench the bridle away from Nick. Her efforts only made Miriah more nervous. "Please *let go*. You're frightening my mare."

"No! You're just an amateur, Tracy. You don't realize the danger."

"I'll be careful."

"The hell you say!"

"Will you stop swearing at me?"

Tiny pinpricks of light seemed to flicker in his eyes as Tracy watched him try to tamp down the more volatie edges of his anger. "All right. I can be reasonable. So, tell me, have you ever done this before?"

"Yes!" She thrust out her chin belligerently.

"When?" He waited, his grip tightened on the bridle.

That nailed her. She dropped her gaze. "Well, it was a while ago."

"How long? When you were growing up on that tiny spread up in Mount Shasta?" he guessed shrewdly.

"Well, what if it was?" she threw back. "Why don't you leave me alone? You don't give a hoot about me, Nick Roberts, you've made that abundantly clear, so don't start pretending now." She yanked on the reins.

If possible, Nick's scowl deepened. "For the last time, Tracy, *get off this horse.*"

Heartache and fury and adrenaline gathered and built inside Tracy until she angrily blurted the first thing that came to mind. "If you're so all-fired determined to get me off, why don't you *take* me off?"

At her words the flickering light in Nick's eyes burst into flame. With his free hand he pulled his Stetson low over his eyes and muttered, "You asked for it."

To her horror, Tracy found herself hauled out of the saddle as if she were merely a fifty-pound sack of potatoes. Adding insult to injury, Nick slung her over his shoulder into an inelegant position that presented her rump skyward.

"You—you *ornery cuss*!" she screeched, burning with embarrassment. She kicked ineffectually and pounded on Nick's back. Yet even as she struggled, she knew she was making no headway. His thick sheepskin jacket protected him from the elements as well as from one small woman's blows.

Vaguely, she was aware of Nick handing over Miriah's reins to the dumbfounded teenager and of him striding away from the arena. "Put me down," she commanded him, breathless.

"Not yet," he told her, still walking. As they passed David, Nick called to him, "Tracy and I need some privacy."

"We can see that," David replied, grinning.

Nick grunted as Tracy landed a well-placed blow at his midsection. "Well, see to it we're not disturbed."

"Count on me, brother," David answered. The boys were staring, openly awed at the spectacle. Eliza wore a satisfied, smug expression.

Gritting her teeth, Tracy tried to kick again but found her legs captured by Nick's arm. "Where are you taking me?" she demanded.

"You'll see."

When Nick's long, ground-eating stride had carried them well away from the arena to where a small grouping of shade trees and benches were sheltered from curious eyes, he finally eased Tracy down.

But instead of putting her on the ground, Nick lowered them onto a bench and held Tracy across his lap. One arm supported her back, the other imprisoned her waist. He was far too strong for her; she couldn't get away if she tried. So she didn't. "There," he said, settling back. "That's better."

Tracy attempted to glare at him but knew she was failing. She was the tiniest bit relieved she hadn't had to go through with the competition, even at the expense of her own dignity. She ought to be angry, she told herself, unable to meet Nick's eyes. But she admitted to herself that by that point it had been only pride prompting her to argue. By then she'd already learned what she'd wanted to know.

And now she was hopelessly aware that to be cradled in Nick's lap was a wonderful place to be.

At last she found her voice. "Why are you doing this?"

"What's the matter? Aren't you comfortable?" His cowboy-tough grin crept up one cheek as he pretended to shift her into a more relaxed position.

She raised her eyes, only to meet the warmest, caring smile she'd ever sen. Her breath caught. For a long moment she simply stared, "Oh, Nick, you have to know I'm not strong around you. I can't—I can't resist you," she admitted softly.

Nick merely nodded, studying her. "Glad to hear it," he finally said.

"'Glad to hear it!'" she repeated, stiffening, "Why that's the cruelest—"

"Cause I want you to be my wife. And I want my wife hot for me."

"—most insensitive thing I've ever..." Tracy's voice trailed off, and she gaped at him. "Excuse me? I thought you said—"

"You heard me." Nick's arms tightened on her waist. "I won't take no for an answer, either. I've got you in my arms and you're not getting out until you agree. So don't try any of your damn-fool arguments!"

"Arguments?" she parroted, slumping against his chest.

"That's right. I can see them forming in those river-green eyes of yours right now, but don't bother. I've got the answers to any barriers you try and set up. I've pretty much given up rodeoing, and I got over my uh...problem about trusting women—thanks to you. So, from your point of view I guess that makes me just about perfect, huh?" His devil-may-care eyes twinkled mischievously.

"No." Tracy felt a misty smile forming. The heavy wind had gentled to a light breeze. It soothed over her skin as soft and comforting as a lover's touch. "You're far from perfect. You've got a hair-trigger temper, you're opinionated, overbearing, domineering—"

"But just right for you?"

Tracy busied herself by fiddling with the soft lining of the jacket covering his chest. She evaded his question until he gave her a little shake. "Aren't I?" he demanded, then surprised her by burying his face in her neck. "Please, Tracy, say it. Because I know as sure as the sun's gonna shine that you're perfect for me."

He lifted his head and gazed at her with agonized eyes. "This morning when you said you were leaving I went into shock. I thought about not having you around when I get home every day. I thought about how hard I've tried to keep away from you when all I've wanted to do is feel you—like this—against me. I'm caught, Trace, in a trap of my own making. I can't let you go."

He drew a difficult breath as if gathering himself. With great conviction he said, "I want you in my bed. I want you to be my wife. I want to daddy your boys. With you I want everything."

Tracy smiled tremulously, struggling to believe it all. "Quite a speech for a laconic cowboy."

"Don't tease," Nick said. "Not now."

She placed a loving hand along his hard cheek. "Okay."

"So, will you? Will you marry me?"

"Your offer sounds tempting. But I don't know about..."

"About, what?" he said impatiently.

"I'm not sure I can marry a man who doesn't love me."

The look of pure shock that crossed Nick's craggy features was balm to her soul. "Dammit, that's what I've been telling you," he assured her in a near shout. "Aren't you listening? I'm crazy about you, Tracy. I want you, I need you, I...love you. There," he finished grumpily. "Are you happy?"

"Oh, yes, Nick," she sighed into his shoulder. "And I love you, too." She wound eager arms around his neck and offered him her lips. He took them in a thrilling, luxurious kiss that did her heart good.

Much later Tracy drew away, trembling with desire and happiness and relief. She said the first thing that came to mind. "Eliza's asked me to continue on as nanny so she can go back to work."

He shrugged, never taking rapt eyes off her face. "As far as I'm concerned you can do anything you want. Except—" he touched her nose "—except barrel race."

She chuckled, loving the feel of his strong arms around her. "You drive a hard bargain. But I have a few negotiating points we need to clarify, as well. Two, to be exact."

"No more bronc busting?" he asked softly.

"Right. At least not on the circuit, okay? I won't mind if you want to compete occasionally around here. It'd be wrong to pressure you to quit completely, I know that now."

"Mmm," Nick murmured, nuzzling her neck. "Are you gonna let the other shoe drop?"

Tracy smiled. It was a very small, very enigmatic smile, one full of feminine mystery. She settled herself more comfortably in Nick's lap and made sure she had full eye contact. "There *is* one more thing I want from you, cowboy."

"Well?"

"I was wondering...hoping...that is..."

"What is it, Tracy? What do you want?"

"A baby," she blurted out.

She suffered through his joyous laughter until his chuckles died away and only a broad grin split his face. He hugged her so tight she couldn't breathe. Then, in his gruff way he told her, "Ma'am, it'd be my pleasure."

* * * * *

Silhouette Romance®

COMING NEXT MONTH

#718 SECOND TIME LUCKY—Victoria Glenn
A Diamond Jubilee Book!
Ailing Aunt Lizbeth glowed with health after Miles Crane kissed her man-shy goddaughter Lara MacEuan. If Miles had his way, his frail aunt would be on a rapid road to recovery!

#719 THE NESTING INSTINCT—Elizabeth August
Zeke Wilson's cynical view of love had him propose a marriage of convenience to Meg Delany. Could his in-name-only bride conceal her longing for a marriage of love?

#720 MOUNTAIN LAUREL—Donna Clayton
Laurel Morgan went to the mountains for rest and relaxation... but Ranger Michael Walker knew fair game when he saw it! The hunt was on, but who was chasing whom?

#721 SASSAFRAS STREET—Susan Kalmes
Callie Baker was furious when the man who outbid her at an antique auction turned out to be Nick Logan, her new boss. Nick, on the other hand, was thrilled....

#722 IN THE FAMILY WAY—Melodie Adams
Fiercely independent divorcée Sarah Jordan was quite in the family way—and had no plans for marriage. But smitten Steven Carlisle had plans of his own—to change her mind!

#723 THAT SOUTHERN TOUCH—Stella Bagwell
Workaholic Whitney Drake ran from her fast-paced New York life to the Louisiana bayou—and right into the arms of Caleb Jones. But could his loving touch convince her to stay forever?

AVAILABLE THIS MONTH:

#712 HARVEY'S MISSING
Peggy Webb

#713 JUST YOU AND ME
Rena McKay

#714 MONTANA HEAT
Dorsey Kelley

#715 A WOMAN'S TOUCH
Brenda Trent

#716 JUST NEIGHBORS
Marcine Smith

#717 HIS BRIDE TO BE
Lisa Jackson

SILHOUETTE® Desire™

MAN OF THE MONTH

SCANDAL'S CHILD
ANN MAJOR

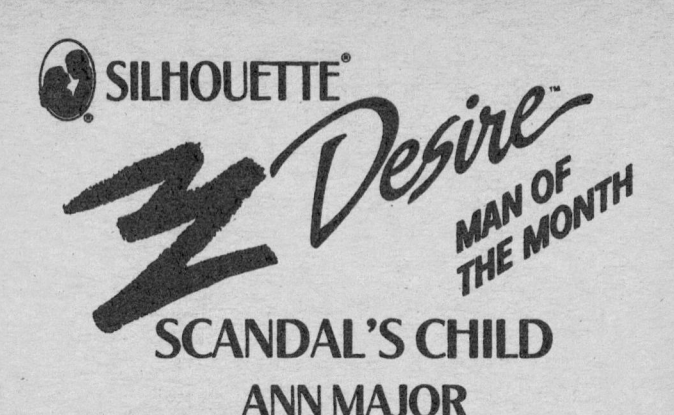

When passion and fate intertwine...

Garret Cagan and Noelle Martin had grown up together in the mysterious bayous of Louisiana. Fate had wrenched them apart, but now Noelle had returned. Garret was determined to resist her sensual allure, but he hadn't reckoned on his desire for the beautiful scandal's child.

Don't miss SCANDAL'S CHILD by Ann Major, Book Five in the Children of Destiny Series, available now at your favorite retail outlet.

Or order your copy of SCANDAL'S CHILD, plus any of the four previous titles in this series (PASSION'S CHILD, #445, DESTINY'S CHILD, #451, NIGHT CHILD, #457 and WILDERNESS CHILD, *Man of the Month* #535), by sending your name, address, zip or postal code, along with a check or money order for $2.50 plus 75¢ postage and handling for each book ordered, payable to Silhouette Reader Service to:

In the U.S.	In Canada
901 Fuhrmann Blvd.	P.O. Box 609
P.O. Box 1396	Fort Erie, Ontario
Buffalo, NY 14269-1396	L2A 5X3

Please specify book titles with your order.

SCAN-1A

You'll flip... your pages won't!
Read paperbacks *hands-free* with

Book Mate • I

The perfect "mate" for all your romance paperbacks

Traveling • Vacationing • At Work • In Bed • Studying • Cooking • Eating

Perfect size for all standard paperbacks, this wonderful invention makes reading a pure pleasure! Ingenious design holds paperback books OPEN and FLAT so even wind can't ruffle pages — leaves your hands free to do other things. Reinforced, wipe-clean vinyl-covered holder flexes to let you turn pages without undoing the strap... supports paperbacks so well, they have the strength of hardcovers!

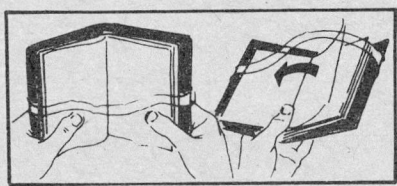

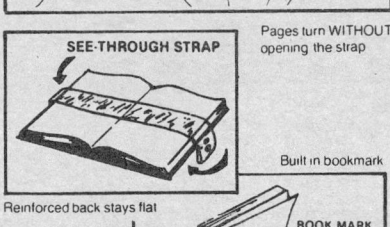

Pages turn WITHOUT opening the strap

SEE-THROUGH STRAP

Reinforced back stays flat

Built in bookmark

BOOK MARK

BACK COVER HOLDING STRIP

10 x 7¼ opened
Snaps closed for easy carrying, too

Available now. Send your name, address, and zip code, along with **a check** or money order for just $5.95 + 75¢ for postage & handling (for a **total of** $6.70) payable to Reader Service to:

Reader Service
Bookmate Offer
901 Fuhrmann Blvd.
P.O. Box 1396
Buffalo, N.Y. 14269-1396

Offer not available in Canada
* New York and Iowa residents add appropriate sales tax.

BM-G

Silhouette Romances

DIAMOND JUBILEE CELEBRATION!

It's Silhouette Books' tenth anniversary, and what better way to celebrate than to toast *you*, our readers, for making it all possible. Each month in 1990, we'll present you with a DIAMOND JUBILEE Silhouette Romance written by an all-time favorite author!

Welcome the new year with *Ethan*—a LONG, TALL TEXANS book by Diana Palmer. February brings Brittany Young's *The Ambassador's Daughter*. Look for *Never on Sundae* by Rita Rainville in March, and in April you'll find *Harvey's Missing* by Peggy Webb. Victoria Glenn, Lucy Gordon, Annette Broadrick, Dixie Browning and many more have special gifts of love waiting for you with their DIAMOND JUBILEE Romances.

Be sure to look for the distinctive DIAMOND JUBILEE emblem, and share in Silhouette's celebration. Saying thanks has never been so romantic....

SRJUB-1